VIRAL

T.A. Berkeley

For T.N. and B.A., my ever-supportive life partners.

CHAPTER ONE

The dark blue Chevy Suburban barreled west on I-66 in the fading daylight, passing close to Manassas, Virginia. A rainproof storage bag, practically bursting at the seams, was strapped to the roof, straps vibrating in the air that rushed over them. The vehicle itself was full as well, with eight occupants filling all the seats, and bags and backpacks wedged into every available spot.

The driver slouched comfortably and held the wheel with one hand, occasionally pushing his thick honey-blond hair off his forehead, though it immediately resettled there each time. If his friends had been looking at him closely, they might have noticed a tense set to his jaw, a slight ripple in his cheek as he clenched his teeth.

His friends, however, weren't paying attention to him. The boy in the front passenger seat was tapping a pack of Camels against his palm. He ripped off the cellophane and slid a cigarette between his lips with a practiced motion, then cracked the window, letting in a rushing, whistling burst of air. He cocked his head to the right to check himself out in the side mirror before flipping the top off a small silver lighter.

Directly behind him, a smoothly muscled girl with blond-streaked hair sprawled in her seat, typing on her phone. She barely acknowledged the driver when he called back, "Kinsey, you better not be posting where we're going."

To Kinsey's left sat another girl, pale and small-boned with chin-length dark hair, leaning on the shoulder of the boy in the far left middle seat. His head inclined over hers in a comforting pose, his cheek resting on her hair. With one of his hands, he fidgeted with a thick silver thumb ring, the movement making the ring glint in the light of the setting sun.

While the first two rows of passengers were largely silent, the three girls in the backseat chattered away. In the middle, a lanky, dark-skinned girl with large, expressive eyes held a tablet and scrolled back and forth, while the other two craned their necks to see. "I don't know. This whole set of poems here is so depressing. It sucks the life out of you after a while. Shouldn't we move them around to break it up a little?"

"Or get rid of a couple," the girl on her right said, absentmindedly tucking a shock of her curly hair, short on the sides and longer on top, behind her right ear. Her knee stayed pressed against the middle girl's.

"Like mine?" said the girl on the other side. Her long dark hair hung down on either side, concealing her expression.

The girl in the middle patted her shoulder. "Definitely not, Rose."

The driver peered at the middle girl in his rearview mirror. "Jesus, Marla, you guys ever stop? School's closed. The magazine can wait."

Marla met his eyes in the reflection. "But we'll get so far behind if we don't keep working. It's due to the printer in a month, and the website and app need to be ready to go in six weeks. What the fuck are we gonna do if school stays closed that whole time?"

"I just meant maybe you could take a few days off and relax," he said. "Is one or two days going to make that much difference?"

The front passenger broke in as if he hadn't noticed them talking. "Derek, how come you never told me about this place? How does your dad have a fucking house in the middle of nowhere and we've never gone there to get shitfaced and laid?"

"Bobby, you really need a special place to get shitfaced and laid?" the driver shot back good-naturedly.

"I'm just saying, I've taken you to *our* vacation house almost every summer."

"Yeah, well, this isn't a family type place. I've only been a couple times myself. It's like a hunting lodge. Not really what I'm into. He's never let me go without him before."

"So why are we going now?"

"He doesn't know *you're* coming. If he did, he'd kill me. But he's got a lot going on right now at work and stuff, so I don't think he'll figure anything out."

"I'm so fucking glad to be getting away from home," the small girl in the middle row said. "Something really fucked up is going on, huh, Lars?"

"Totally," the boy leaning on her was quick to agree. "No one is buying this asbestos cleanup story. It's just making everything seem shadier."

Kinsey looked up from her phone for the first time since the trip started. "Oh shit, what if it's to hide some teacher scandal? I wonder who'll be gone when school opens again."

"Mr. Pruitt," at least three of them chimed in simultaneously, and the entire vehicle rang with laughter.

"Oh, how we'll miss his pocket masturbating and child-molester haircut," Marla said.

Everyone laughed harder at this except Rose. "I don't think that's it," she said quietly. "It's worse. I don't know what, but something really bad is happening."

"Nah," said Marla. "Just general incompetence and overreaction to something stupid. You watch. Things'll go back to normal, and we'll never know why they closed. They'll be too embarrassed to say anything."

The girl on her other side nodded, her mop of curly hair bouncing. "But Derek has a point: we shouldn't work the whole time we're off. I mean, it's only two months till graduation. Shit's about to get real; who knows when we'll be able to relax again? I've got to get a job this summer to save some money, and then it's like, here we go." She squeezed Marla's hand. "Off to different states."

Marla sighed and tucked the tablet into a small backpack. "Yeah, okay, Diane." She kissed the other girl's cheek and nuzzled her briefly.

Bobby said from the front seat, "Besides, save it for when you're really bored out in Buttfuck, West Virginia. Once the drugs run out, we'll probably all want to work on the magazine just to keep from killing ourselves."

"I don't think reading poetry is going to make you not want to kill yourself, Bobby," Diane said. Laughter rang through the car again, and she looked surprised and pleased at the reaction.

Kinsey looked up from her phone. "I need to pee," she said abruptly.

"Me too," several others chimed in.

Derek looked in the rearview mirror at his friends, then ahead again. "There's a truck stop. I'm not in a hurry to get to the lodge anyway."

A towering neon sign grew closer. "Lazy T's," it read, above a cartoonish cowboy holding a branding iron with a slanted capital T on it in one hand, a beer bottle in the other.

The setting sun was getting redder and more glaring through the windshield. Derek eased the SUV next to a gas pump, cut off the motor, and got out.

Bobby leaned out his window and gestured at Lazy T's, a few hundred feet away. The neon beer flashed in three different positions, tipping toward the cowboy's mouth over and over. "Dude, let's go get a few before we leave."

Derek looked at it, then back at the car, and said in a low tone, "Make sure everyone's got an ID."

Bobby turned and surveyed the back. His eyes passed over Kinsey to Lars and the girl next to him. "ID? ID?" They both nodded. He looked past them to the third row. "Ladies?"

Rose said, "Yeah, I have one." Marla wrinkled her nose. "Um, I guess Di and I are officially the biggest nerds in the car."

"Seriously?" Bobby said with an eye roll.

Diane shrugged and pointed in the opposite direction of the bar. "Don't worry, there's a diner. We can hang out there until you guys are done."

Derek finished pumping gas and drove to the entrance of the restaurant to drop the girls off. "Text me if you get bored before we get out," he said. Lars got out and pulled his seat forward so they could climb out. Marla stumbled, and Lars grabbed her hand to steady her. "Bye," he said with a smile that coaxed grins from both girls. He jumped back in and the SUV pulled off, back through the gas station and over to the bar parking lot.

"I'm going to go ahead and say it," Marla murmured. "He is so damn hot."

"Hey!" Diane said in mock protest, but she was smiling. She grabbed Marla's hand and pulled her toward the glass door. "It's true, Monique is a lucky, lucky girl. Almost as lucky as me."

"I think they're just friends," Marla said.

"Really?"

"Yeah, they're just really, really close. Been friends for, like, ever."

"Well, I don't know how somebody like that stays single," Diane marveled. "Either of them, really! But Lars especially."

Marla gave her a peck on the cheek. "Okay, let's try to keep our hands off each other. We don't know what kind of place this is." Diane nodded glumly and dropped her hand.

* * *

In the bar, the rest of the group found a corner booth. The waitress barely raised an eyebrow at any of the IDs and brought a round of drinks. Bobby got a shot of whiskey and downed it immediately, chasing it with a swig of beer.

The waitress soon returned with baskets of fries and jalapeno poppers and set them in the middle of the table. Everyone dug in, blowing on the piping hot food and transferring it from hand to hand to cool it off; all except Kinsey, once again bent over her phone again, one hand holding her wine glass absently, and Rose, who was staring off into the distance.

Monique nibbled on a fry, washed it down with wine, and asked, "So, have any of you heard whether they're going to add days to the school year when they reopen?"

That got Kinsey's attention. "How would that work with graduation?" she asked, aggrieved at the idea. "Maybe they could let the seniors off and make the rest of those little fuckers do extra time."

"They'll work something out," Lars said. "At most they'd make us do some extra credit after graduation to make it official before they send the real diplomas. Doubt they'll even do that."

Rose stirred and brought her focus back to the table. "That's if they reopen at all this year. What happens if they don't?"

"Fu-uck," Kinsey groaned.

Derek took a long pull of his beer and set the glass onto the table. "Well, whatever's going on, if it's that serious, losing part of our summer isn't going to seem like a big deal."

The others all looked at him. Rose shivered a little. In the brief silence, Derek craned his head to look for the waitress. "If you want another round, better order it. I got three more hours of driving, so I'm good with this one." His expression was blandly pleasant. The tensing and relaxing of his jaw was imperceptible under the bar's dim lights.

* * *

The other two girls were still working on their own basket of fries when Derek texted Marla to let her know he was ready to get on the road again. They sucked down the rest of their Diet Cokes and left money on top of the check. The SUV was idling by the curb when they got outside. Once again Lars jumped out to let them slide back into the third row.

It was nearly dark; there was barely a glow left from the faded sunset. The last few lights of the truck stop slid by the windows as they got back onto the highway.

Two hours later, the vehicle passed a sign, "Welcome to wild and wonderful West Virginia," with little fanfare from any of its occupants. Radio stations came and went;

when all they could get was country music or religious sermons, Lars offered his phone. Bobby hooked it into the car stereo, and a mix of vintage funk and underground hip-hop carried the car through mountains and small towns.

On a two-lane highway with few cars driving in either direction, Bobby reached into the black messenger bag between his feet and opened a pen case. Several joints were nestled inside. He got his lighter from his pants pocket and lit one up.

After a few hits he offered it to Derek, who hesitated, shrugged, then took it with his free hand. He took a small hit and raised the joint. "Anyone else?"

Monique reached between the seat backs and plucked it from his hand, inhaled, and offered it to Lars, but he motioned toward Kinsey. "You first," he said. She grabbed it and sucked in two quick hits, holding her breath on the second one as she passed the joint back to Lars.

When Lars held it toward the back seat, Marla took it and looked at it. "Maybe another time." She looked at Diane, who shook her head. Marla offered it to Rose instead. She started to inhale, then coughed abruptly and sputtered, "Shit!" Marla thumped her back a couple times. Bobby and Kinsey laughed. "Pass it up here, amateur!" Bobby called.

Rose pinched the end between her fingers, hissing with pain. "Derek, take the next turn you can and cut your lights."

CHAPTER TWO

"What did you say?" Derek turned down the music.

A set of mailboxes with luminescent numbers appeared ahead of them, marking a small rocky lane between sets of thick trees. "Turn right now. There!" Rose's barking tone sounded so unlike her that Derek obeyed.

"Now turn everything off! The lights! The music!" Rose cried. Derek did as she said.

Everyone was quiet in the sudden darkness. "What's wrong, Rose?" Derek asked in a half whisper.

Bobby started to chime in. "Yeah, what the—"

She shushed them forcefully, and everyone sat in bewildered silence. A minute later, lights and a muffled car sound passed by on the highway, and Rose exhaled. "Just wait a sec, then we can go," she said. "That was a cop. He was gonna pull us over. But he didn't see us turn down here."

Several voices spoke at once, their incredulous questions tangled together in the close, dark interior.

Rose broke in, and her firm tone silenced them momentarily. "I saw something and I knew it was a cop car. I don't know how; I just knew right away. If he caught us and searched our stuff—"

"Shit, paranoid much?" Bobby said. "There's no way—there's just no—" He spluttered and trailed off.

"Anyway, he's gone now," Rose said. As their eyes adjusted to the darkness, the others stared at her face, a mask of calm. "We can go."

Derek turned in his seat, his face barely visible. "But if it was—I don't see how we could be sure, but if it was—wouldn't he come back to try to see where the car went? What if he passed us on the way back?"

"He won't," Rose said. Her confidence faltered and she added, "I mean, I don't think that'll happen."

Kinsey broke in. "Let's just go. She's full of shit anyway. She didn't see anyone; it was just a coincidence, that car coming by when it did."

Eventually Derek started the car again and backed out onto the road. It was empty so he resumed driving, obeying the speed limit precisely. Bobby didn't light another joint, and the music was quieter than before. A heavy mood hung over the car for the remainder of the journey. Gradually, the combination of alcohol, pot, and the rhythmic cadence of the music caused most of them to doze off.

Derek turned off the highway onto a smaller road that curved through countryside with only the occasional house or barn to punctuate the darkness. He flipped on his high beams and slowed, squinting at each street sign as it appeared in the light. Finally he turned left onto a single-lane road that wound through trees on either side, going slower still for about a mile. At an unmarked road, he turned left again.

The new road was paved for twenty feet, then turned to gravel. It dipped downward, and he stopped at a gate that blocked the road. He got out, and the slight chill in the air and sudden stillness of the car woke his passengers. Derek tapped a code on a padlock and it sprang open; unhooking the gate, he walked it forward until the road was clear. He drove the SUV a few feet and stopped again to close the gate behind them.

Soon the road changed again. The gravel they left seemed smooth in comparison to the steep, rocky, uneven surface they bumped down for the last leg of the journey. The headlights illuminated a small wooden bridge over what must have been a creek, though high plants obscured its banks. Then they reached a gravel area in front of a wooden house.

Derek left the headlights on as everyone blearily stumbled from the truck. The air was chilly and damp. Frogs and crickets creaked and sang shrilly in the darkness. Derek led the way up three wooden steps to the porch that ran the length of the house and opened the front door. He smiled back at his friends, but weariness and a trace of worry dimmed his usual charm.

"Come on in," he said.

* * *

The mood was subdued as they started hauling bags of clothes and food into the house. But Derek started a blaze in the living room fireplace, and the inviting light, warmth, and the scent of the burning logs seemed to lift everyone's spirits.

Lars hooked his phone to a small set of portable speakers and put on an upbeat mix of seventies funk. He found a liquor cabinet and small fridge and began pouring drinks.

The rest explored the house. The lodge had looked small against the towering trees that surrounded it, but inside its impressive size was clear. On the main floor, a large open room contained two couches and several large, cozy armchairs, all facing the fireplace. Behind it, a long plank table lined with padded benches, an ornate wooden chair at either end, separated the living room from the kitchen.

"At least there aren't deer heads and bearskins everywhere," Monique said as she came back into the main area.

There were several small side rooms on the first floor; a bathroom, an office, and a bedroom with a single bed. Near the front door was a sturdy wooden staircase leading to the second floor. That level consisted of a four large bedrooms and another bathroom. Each of the two couples settled on a room upstairs. "Someone's going to have to double up," Derek said apologetically to the rest of his friends.

"Lars and I will," Monique said right away. She giggled and looked at him. "It'll be like the old days!"

"Mo and I used to have sleepovers all the time," Lars told the others. "Until we turned like twelve, and our parents decided it was too weird."

Derek offered the fourth upstairs bedroom to Rose. "Oh, that's okay," she said. "You should have the last big room since it's your place, kind of. Besides, I'd rather stay downstairs. I stay up really late and I love this fireplace."

The group unpacked and put away their things with varying thoroughness. They returned to the main room by ones and twos. Lars mixed more drinks, and Bobby passed a second joint.

Marla hesitated again but took a couple hits this time. Diane still demurred, saying she shouldn't mix alcohol with pot. Hearing that, Lars jumped up and fixed her another drink instead. She smiled as she took it, her cheeks flushed from the first one she'd had. She took the glass and raised it toward Derek. "Thanks for freeing us from Woodbridge for a while. I was starting to feel like I was on house arrest."

"Yeah, thanks, man!" Lars said.

Derek smiled slightly. "No worries," he said. "Whatever's going on, I just wanted to be around friends and get away from it. Glad you all could make it."

"So what was everyone's story with their parents?" Marla asked. "My cousin in Bowling Green covered for me and told my parents I was going there to visit. They won't check in; they hate to seem overprotective."

Diane chimed in, "I told my mom and dad I was going with Marla, and I *accidentally* wrote the number down wrong and forgot my charger." She grinned. "They won't question it; I've never done anything like this before. But hey, I have to do something rebellious before graduation, right?"

"What about you guys?" Marla asked Kinsey and Bobby.

He leaned back on the couch, his arm around his girlfriend. "Told 'em I was taking this foxy bitch to Virginia Beach."

Kinsey jabbed an elbow into his side. "My dad's away on business in China all month, and my mom's over there visiting him for a week, so I didn't have to tell them anything." She pulled her phone from her back pocket. "Fuck! I keep forgetting there's no reception here."

Rose smiled. "My mom thinks I'll be with my dad for a while. She won't call because she doesn't like talking to him. Long as I text her once or twice I'll be fine." She looked at Derek. "We can get reception somewhere, right?"

He shrugged. "I mean, we're kind of in a hole in the ground here. If we get to one of the towns, I bet we'll be okay."

Marla looked at Lars and Monique, who were cuddling on the rug near the fireplace, Lars's back propped against the leg of an armchair. "And you two? How did you get to come?"

Lars chuckled. "Said Mo wanted to go on a road trip to Graceland. I hope one of you can fake photos for us when we get back." Everyone laughed.

"Derek, what did you tell your dad?" Marla asked.

Derek shrugged. "He knows I'm here. He just wouldn't like me bringing anyone else. You know, worried about lawsuits and shit. Minors overdosing on his property or whatever." He stood. "See you tomorrow, guys." He climbed the wooden stairs to a chorus of goodnights.

Without Derek in the room, the gathering felt less cohesive. The silences grew longer, and little by little, the group thinned. Marla and Diane were the first to go upstairs. They closed the door to their bedroom, and Diane threw her arms around Marla.

"Our first night together where we don't have to pretend it's a sleepover," Diane said into Marla's ear, and giggled. "Also I feel a little drunk." Their lips met and parted, tongues circling each other's mouths as Diane began lifting the hem of Marla's T-shirt. They stepped apart long enough for her to pull it over Marla's head. Then they kissed again, Diane's hands stroking Marla's back and slowly working at her bra clasp until it popped open.

Marla stepped back, letting the bra fall from her small soft breasts, then lay on the bed. The lights were off, but moonlight coming through the window gave just enough illumination for them to see one another.

Diane straddled Marla, bent down, and kissed her full lips, trailing her mouth down her neck to trace the bones palpable under the skin of her chest. Marla gasped and arched her back. The rest of their clothes soon found their way to the floor. Diane lowered herself between Marla's thighs, nestling her mouth into the soft crevice. Marla moaned out loud, then pressed her hand to her mouth and breathed more quietly.

Diane's tongue quickened its movements. She buried her face more deeply into Marla's warmth, occasionally coming up for a gasping breath before diving back in. Marla's thighs began to grip her head involuntarily. Diane pulled back slightly so she could slip two fingers in. Soft heat surrounded them as she moved them in and out quickly.

Marla's excitement came to a fever pitch and she grabbed Diane's hair as waves coursed through her and gradually slowed.

Diane pulled herself up to lie next to Marla, who only rested for a few moments. She gently licked one of Diane's nipples, and her entire body responded to the delicate stimulation. Marla's hand moved to the other breast and brushed it lightly. Diane grew quiet and still, lost in the sensations, and her own hand moved down between her legs. It was less than five minutes before she came with a little gasp, arching her back. Marla claimed her lips in a kiss.

Afterwards, Diane grew still, lost in the lingering sensations. "How do you connect to me so easily?" she finally whispered. "No one's ever really been able to make me feel anything before. You know?"

"It's so easy," Marla murmured. "You tell me exactly what you want. It's just no one was paying close enough attention before."

They wriggled under the covers and lay in an embrace. Outside the door, they heard creaking on the stairs and floorboards as some of the others went to their bedrooms. In the room on the other side of the wall, bedsprings creaked.

"Shit," said Diane in a whisper. "I think that's Bobby and Kinsey's room. God I hope I don't have to hear anything from them on this trip."

Marla giggled. "I don't think you're going to be that lucky."

Diane groaned. "I find him so repulsive, and she wouldn't give me the time of day if she didn't have to be nice to me because you and Bobby are friends."

"Well," Marla said, "he and I aren't friends so much as coworkers. At speech tournaments, you want to be able to hang out with everyone so you don't go crazy waiting for your turn."

"Yeah, but you get along with everyone," Diane said, sounding envious. "You're like some politician walking through the halls at school. 'Hey so-and-so, how's that paper coming along? Oh, I hope your mom's feeling better.'"

Marla poked her in the ribs. "It doesn't mean anything. It's just something I do. You're different, though; when you talk to someone, it means something. It's special." They kissed some more.

Just then, the same bedsprings they'd heard before started to creak again, rhythmically and repeatedly this time. Diane's eyes widened in exaggerated horror, and Marla snorted with laughter. She broke away and buried her face in a pillow to muffle her giggles. Diane smiled too and whispered into Marla's ear, "I guess I can't be mad about anyone doing what makes them happy right now, even if it's Bobby and Kinsey."

* * *

The next morning, Diane and Marla were the first to stir on the second floor. They tiptoed into the bathroom and showered together, then dressed in jeans and flannel shirts and went downstairs. Diane fiddled with the unfamiliar coffee maker until she got it going, then rummaged in the pantry and fridge.

She and Marla were polishing off some French toast when Rose emerged from the small main-floor bedroom. She had dark smudges under her eyes, as if she'd gone to bed without taking off her makeup.

"Want some?" Diane asked with her mouth full, gesturing at the last few bites on her plate. "I can make more."

"No, I'm okay," Rose said. She poured herself a cup of coffee, added milk and sugar, and drank it in silence while Marla did dishes. Diane suggested a walk, and the other two agreed.

They left the lodge and paused on the porch to survey their surroundings. Beyond the small yard and the gravel area where the SUV was parked, hills rose all around them, some covered with grassy meadows that looked mowed or grazed on, others thick with forest. The craggy road Derek had navigated the night before climbed sharply upward and disappeared into a grove of trees. Diane hesitated, wondering which way they should walk, and how much of the land belonged to Derek's father.

"I don't know," Rose said.

"What?" Diane was puzzled.

Rose shrugged. "I don't know which hill we should go up," she said.

"I was just wondering that myself," Diane said. The girls stepped off the porch and walked around to the back of the house. The slope seemed less steep than the others.

They started to climb. In less than ten minutes they reached the top, a flat meadow surrounded by woods. They wandered through a stand of trees. After a few minutes, Rose broke the silence. "So what do you guys think about Bobby and Kinsey?" she asked.

Diane snorted, remembering the creaking of the night before. Rose smiled too. "They've got that going for them," she said.

"What?" Diane asked.

Rose said, "That they're so into each other."

Diane nodded slowly, looking confused again.

"He's dangerous, though," Rose said.

"What do you mean?" Marla asked.

Rose spoke with certainty. "When he gets mad, he gets violent. At least he thinks about it. He just doesn't act on it. He doesn't really want to hurt people, but in a way he kinda does."

"Really?" said Marla. "Have you seen him hit anyone?"

"No," said Rose.

"Then why do you think that?"

Rose shrugged. "I don't know. Never mind."

"Well, I wouldn't be surprised," Diane said. "Bobby is a total asshole. Derek seems so nice. I wonder why he dragged Bobby along."

"I don't think he can really see the truth about him," Rose said confidently. "He likes him too much."

Diane started to answer, but Marla said, "You mean *likes him* likes him?"

"Oh!" Diane said. Then "Really? I don't get that vibe off of Derek at all."

Marla rolled her eyes. "You said the same exact thing about me the day after we hooked up for the first time."

Diane blushed and giggled. "Well, that's true," she said. "But did you ever get that impression from Derek?"

Marla shook her head. "He's the kind of person who doesn't make you think about it either way, isn't he?"

"I guess it makes sense," Diane said. "But how long have you thought that, Rose?"

"Well, I've known Derek liked guys for a while," she said. "He doesn't talk about it much, even to me—I don't know if it's his dad, or just being private. But about his crush on Bobby? Not long. I only figured it out in the car on the way here."

They reached a clearing with the remains of a low stone wall or house foundation poking through some weeds, and the three girls perched on it to rest.

"Well," Marla said, "As long as we're gossiping, any opinions about Lars?" Her voice warmed as she said his name.

"He's really loyal," Rose said. "Once he cares about someone, like Monique, he'll do anything for them, you know?"

"Well, sure," Diane said. "That's like most people, right?"

"It's different with him," Rose said. "It's always his main priority."

Diane and Marla both stared at her again, as if she were a fascinating lab specimen. She shrugged again and pulled a pack of cigarettes and a plastic lighter from her pocket. She lit up, then inhaled deeply. "Anyway," she said, as if that summed up everything she had been talking about. "Should we start back to the house?"

They got up from the stone ruins and made their way back through the woods, across the hilltop meadow, and to the edge of the hill. Looking down, they could see the lodge and Lars and Monique approaching a long shed at the back of the house.

The girls started down the hill. They saw the two duck into the door of the shed and appear a few seconds later, arms laden with firewood.

The girls caught Lars's eye as he came out of the shed. He balanced the logs on one arm and waved with the other, then had to catch the wood before it slipped from his arms altogether. He looked up again and smiled sheepishly, then he and Monique went back around to the front of the house.

The girls increased their pace as the hill got steeper near the bottom. They practically jogged onto the flat ground, then circled around to the front of the house. Inside, everyone was in the living room. A fire was once again roaring in the hearth, and the three girls suddenly became aware of the chill that had seeped into their hands and feet. They took off their jackets and shoes and crouched near the fireplace, holding their hands out.

"Good walk?" Derek asked.

"Yeah, it's nice here," Diane said. "Lots of hills, though."

"See any deer?"

"Nope, no animals, just a few birds."

"Well, we probably will. The few times I've been here I've seen deer, foxes, lots of rabbits."

"Great," Kinsey said, putting away her phone. She'd once again taken it out absentmindedly, then frowned at it in frustration. "We can sit around waiting for deer to pass by. Hours of fun."

Derek kept his voice upbeat, though there was a note of irritation. "There's a bunch of DVDs in that cabinet. And there's board games and cards."

"And you could always, you know, read a book," Lars said sarcastically. Kinsey rolled her eyes at him.

"We could build a fire outside tonight, have a cookout," Derek offered. "I brought hot dogs and beans—and veggie dogs too," he added, nodding at Lars, who thanked him with a smile.

"What about hunting?" Bobby asked with an air of impatience. "Can we kill some shit while we're here?"

Derek shrugged reluctantly and looked slightly worried. "I mean, if you know how to use a gun, I suppose you could. It's probably not the right season, but we're pretty far out. Probably no one would hear. But what about all the cleaning and butchering?"

"I'm talking about killing for sport, man," Bobby said with a nasty smile.

Lars sighed heavily. "I'm going to read for a while," he said. He climbed the stairs and his footsteps thumped down the hall to his bedroom. Monique gave Bobby a dirty look and pulled the blanket she'd been sharing with Lars to her chin.

"Sounds like a good idea, actually," said Diane. "Reading, I mean." Marla nodded. The girls went to their room.

Rose retrieved a notebook and pen from her room and got back into her jacket, adding a light wool hat and gloves before going outside to sit on the wooden porch swing.

Only Monique, Derek, Bobby, and Kinsey remained in the main room. "Anyone want to go for a walk?" Derek asked, mostly addressing Bobby.

"Okay," Bobby said, looking at Kinsey.

She shrugged, unfolded her long limbs, and stood. "Why the fuck not?" she said. "If I don't do something my muscles are going to turn to flab in this place."

Derek kept his face neutral and looked at Monique. She shook her head and stretched out on the couch.

"Okay, let's go," Derek said. They threw on jackets and shoes and left.

* * *

When the light started to fade from the sky, Derek and Bobby started a fire in a ring of stones in a corner of the yard. Larger stones and part of an old tree trunk provided seating around it.

The others slowly trickled into the circle of light and heat from their various rooms and helped assemble supplies for the hot dog roast. Beer cans were cracked open as the group speared hot dogs and veggie dogs on sticks and held them over the leaping tongues of the fire.

The tension of earlier melted away temporarily, diffused by the fire, a starry night, and beer. Conversation slowed, yet the silences were comfortable. A second twelve-pack appeared as the first one ran low.

During one lull in the conversation, Rose spoke up. "Derek?"

He looked up from his bowl of baked beans.

"You know something about what's going on at home, don't you?"

CHAPTER THREE

The silence became deeper, hushed. Everyone was suddenly attentive. Derek looked down, shoved the spoonful of beans into his mouth, and chewed thoughtfully. No one spoke.

"A little bit," he finally said.

"Wow," Marla said. "Really?"

Derek sighed. "I only know what I heard from . . . a couple of people. Not much." He took a swig of beer, still staring contemplatively into the fire. The group waited quietly until he spoke again. "I heard they closed school because something was going around. Some kind of . . . disease or something."

"Fuck!" Bobby blurted. "Like Ebola or something?"

"Something else," Rose murmured, so quietly that only Diane, who was sitting closest to her, heard it over the crackle of the fire.

"Kind of, I guess," Derek said. "I don't know if it's contagious or deadly, but the school officials were worried enough that they didn't want it to spread any more than it already has."

"Who got it? Anyone you know?" asked Kinsey, the most alert she'd seemed the whole trip.

"Nobody I was close to. A new girl — sophomore, I think? She'd just transferred. And Mary Slivinsky — I had driver's ed with her a couple years ago. Did anyone else know her?"

Marla murmured, "She was in calculus with me last year."

"I heard Danny Ramirez had it too," Derek added. "He's on yearbook; that's all I know about him."

Several of the others nodded in recognition at the name. "Anyone else?" Lars asked quietly.

"I think there were more, but I don't know who. I never noticed anyone dropping out of my classes, did you?" No one answered.

"So what's the disease like? What happens to them?" Bobby asked.

"I don't really know," Derek said. "I just know people have gotten taken out of school really suddenly. I don't know if they're at home, in a hospital, or what."

"Or dead," Rose said, more audibly this time.

Derek tore his eyes away from the fire to look at her. "I don't know what happened to any of them after they left school," he repeated.

"Does anyone remember freshman year, when that kid Dave killed himself?" Monique asked. "And there was a thing during morning announcements, an assembly, they had grief counselors come in, everything? There's no way four kids have died and no one's doing anything."

"Unless they died of something that needs to be kept secret," Rose said.

Kinsey threw her empty beer can as far as she could. "Fuck, Rose, enough! You're freaking us all out! I'm sick of your lame-ass conspiracy theory shit."

Rose looked as if she was going to cry, but she bit her lip and said nothing.

"Don't pick on her," Derek snapped. "She's just trying to figure out what's going on." He looked around. "I didn't hear much, but what I did hear scared the living shit out of me. That's why I wanted to leave. I don't know how contagious it is, or what happens when people get it, or what happens to them after they disappear." He finished his beer and dropped the can on the ground. "This place is kind of off the grid. That sounded good to me right now. On the grid, we might be easier to find if—" He shook his head and fell silent.

"But this is all speculation," Lars said with deliberate calm. "We shouldn't start getting paranoid."

"What about our families?" Monique asked plaintively. "If there's some disease taking over, will our parents be—" She choked back a lump in her throat and didn't finish.

"Or my little brother?" Bobby broke in. "Sammy's a piece of shit, but I don't want anything to happen to him."

"Just people our age," Rose whispered.

"What did you say?" Kinsey was livid.

Rose stayed calm this time. "It only affects people our age."

Derek stared at her, his mouth open a little. "That's what I was thinking. How are you coming up with this stuff?"

Rose shrugged.

"Well, anyway," Derek said, "that's what I think too. I've only heard about students in our school getting it. Not family, not teachers or guidance counselors, nobody else."

"Aren't we talking an extremely small sample size, though?" Lars interjected. "I mean, how long has this been going around? Isn't it too soon to tell? Who knows what's happened even in the day since we've been gone?"

"Yeah," Derek conceded. "It's too soon to tell. If any of you wants to go back and check on your families, I guess we could try to find a car rental place in town."

The group looked at one another across the campfire. For a few long moments, no one said a word. Finally, Lars spoke. "I don't know," he said. "I'm not convinced anything is going on. We've been drinking, it's dark, we're in a strange place. I think we should calm down and talk about it in the morning." He put his arm around Monique and pulled her close; she pressed her face into his neck.

"You're right," said Marla. Diane was clutching her hand. "We shouldn't jump to conclusions tonight. We'll just make dumb decisions we'll probably regret."

There was more silence, and then someone changed the subject. The group started to disperse and head back inside. Derek moved to stamp out the fire, but Rose stopped him. "I'm going to stay awhile," she said. "Don't worry, I'll make sure it's all the way out before I come inside." Derek left the rest of the embers glowing red and quietly went inside and up to his room.

* * *

Everyone awoke earlier than the previous day, except for Bobby, Kinsey, and Rose in her little first-floor room. She didn't stir until after ten thirty.

The others spent a quiet breakfast together. The conversation of the previous night hung in the air, unaddressed as if by unspoken agreement.

Kinsey and Bobby came down at eleven, and his mood immediately set everyone on edge. Kinsey sat at the long table clutching a cup of coffee in one hand and her forehead in the other. Derek finally suggested that the two go into town for supplies. He gave them a shopping list and directions, as well as the combination for the padlocked gate. They didn't take much convincing; after showers and more coffee, Bobby peeled away in the Suburban with Kinsey in the passenger seat.

Once they were safely out of view of the lodge, he asked Kinsey to search his bag for a small Altoids can. Inside was a tiny Ziploc bag half full of white powder. "Set me up, babe?" he asked. Kinsey expertly dipped her pinky finger in and scooped a minute heap of powder onto her manicured fingernail, which she held under one of Bobby's nostrils. She dipped back in and did the other nostril for him, then her own, before stashing the baggie away. "Yeah!" Bobby said, slapping the steering wheel with the palm of his hand.

After thirty minutes of driving and a few more hits of coke, they began to see the occasional gas station and store, and less open land between houses. Another half mile and they were in the small town of Buckhannon.

They saw a bar and restaurant, and Bobby slowed. "Should we get some drinks?" he asked. "And lunch, I guess."

"No, let's wait," Kinsey said. "I won't be able to eat for a while. Let's do the shopping first."

"Fuck that," Bobby said. "I don't feel like running errands for Derek." His thumbs drummed restlessly on the steering wheel and he slowed further, nearly coming to a stop outside the diner.

"Like I do?" Kinsey said. "But I don't want to go back and tell him, 'Oh yeah, we just took your car for a ride to get high and drunk.' Come on, he's your friend."

Bobby groaned. He put his foot on the accelerator, speeding up again. "Okay, where's the fucking store?"

"I don't know, but it's not going to take us long to find it."

Bobby drove through a few more intersections until they came to a supermarket. He parked and they walked in briskly, still coursing with energy. He grabbed a cart, hopping onto the base of it and riding it up and down the aisles. Once Kinsey stopped him long enough to wrestle the grocery list from him, she did the shopping, finding him occasionally to drop more items into the cart as he whizzed by.

She worked her way down the list with mechanical precision, then corralled Bobby and took him to the front of the store, faintly aware of the disapproving locals staring at them. Out in the parking lot, they threw the bags into the back of the truck and got in. "Now, let's get fucked up!" Bobby said, speeding back down the road to the restaurant they'd passed.

Inside, the walls were covered with faux-quirky oddities. A boy about their age, skinny and tall with reddish brown hair, was mopping up a spill by the front counter. A hostess who looked to be in her early twenties showed them to a booth near the back of the room. "Sherry will be over real soon to take your order," she said with a rote smile.

Bobby scanned the front of the menu, then flipped it over. "Here we go," he said. "Cool, they do hard stuff, not just beer. What do you want, babe?"

"I'm good," she said. "I might fuck it up if I drink on top of it. I'm just getting a burger and Coke." She gave out a quick, tight laugh at that.

"Whatever," Bobby said. He put the menu down and craned his head, looking for the waitress. He fidgeted and sighed, drumming his fingers on top of the napkin dispenser. A thirtysomething woman came over five minutes later. Her delicate features seemed too small for her square face. Her frizzy hair was pulled back in a plastic clip.

"Good afternoon. I'm Sherry, and I'll be your server," she said. "What can I get y'all to drink?"

"Diet Coke, please," Kinsey said.

"Yeah, I'll get a shot of whiskey—you got Jameson?—and a Miller Lite," Bobby said.

The waitress raised her eyebrows. "Could I see some ID?" she asked.

"Of course," Bobby said grandly, producing the card from his wallet with a flourish.

The waitress looked at it, then at him. She handed back the card. "I'm sorry, darlin', I can't serve you any liquor. Would you like a soda or some water?"

Bobby's eyes narrowed. "What are you talking about?" he said.

Sherry glanced around, then leaned toward him and lowered her voice. "Look, son, I could call the cops or take away that fake license. Hell, I can see the real one right there in your wallet." She gestured at the leather rectangle, which Bobby had left open; all three could see the corner of another driver's license poking out.

Bobby gritted his teeth. "Just give me the goddamn drink, okay?"

The woman's square jaw hardened. "You want to watch your mouth, young man. I can have you thrown out. I got a son your age, and I'm not about to let a minor drink on my watch, specially one that looks like he's drunk already."

Bobby leaped to his feet. "Oh yeah?" he said loudly. "My dad could buy this fucking restaurant ten times over. I'm going to fucking Princeton next fall. You think not giving me a drink is going to somehow make you better than me, you redneck bitch?" His face inched closer to hers as he spoke. She flushed with anger, but her steely demeanor faltered as she noticed the bright, feverish glow in his eyes.

By this time, several diners were looking at them. Bobby didn't notice, but Kinsey saw a beefy man at the booth across from them staring; he seemed to be weighing whether or not to intervene. "Bobby, let's just go," she said.

Bobby looked at her, then Sherry. He said in an even louder voice, "I. Want. A. Mother. Fucking. Drink!"

The man in the booth started to rise, but before he could, the skinny kid who had been mopping near the door wedged himself between Sherry and Bobby. "Chill out and leave her alone!" he said to Bobby.

Bobby laughed. "What, you protecting your girlfriend? I know she's your mom, but this is West Virginia after all. She could be both. Huh?" He laughed again, a hard, barking sound.

The kid hesitated, outraged but unsure how to proceed. At that moment, a man who looked like he could be a manager approached the group, cellphone in hand. "Son, we're gonna call the police if you don't leave."

"Bobby, come on," Kinsey pleaded. She stood and reached across the table to pull at his arm. He blinked and looked at her, his anger seeming to subside.

"Fine," he said. "Out of my way, you sack of shit!" When the redheaded boy didn't move quickly enough, Bobby shoved him, hard. He stumbled backward and fell against the waitress, who bumped into the corner of another booth.

"Mom!" the boy said, helping Sherry steady herself as Bobby and Kinsey practically ran for the door. "You all right?"

Bobby laughed the whole way to the car. "That was better than whiskey!" he said. "I should've clocked that little shithead. But still!"

Kinsey looked at him with a mixture of anger and affection. "You're such a dick, Bobby."

The SUV careened out of town. On the outskirts, they saw a dingy Subway and stopped for food. They ate as Bobby drove.

As Kinsey wiped her mouth and took a long swallow of Diet Coke, something occurred to her. "How did you know that guy was the waitress's son?"

"What?"

"You said 'I know she's your mom.' I thought you were just saying that to mess with him. But later he called her 'Mom.' How did you know?"

Bobby shrugged. "Pretty obvious, right?"

"How?" Kinsey pressed. "They looked nothing alike. What are the chances?"

Bobby grunted noncommittally. "Maybe it was totally obvious and you're fucked up on coke," he said. "Or maybe it was a lucky guess. Why do you care?"

"It's a little weird is all," she said, partly to herself. She ripped open a bag of chips and pulled out a few, which she chewed contemplatively.

"Whatever," Bobby said through a mouthful of sandwich. "All I know is I still haven't had a drink, and I'm starting to come down. Tell me if you see where we're supposed to turn."

Frowning slightly, Kinsey leaned her head on the back of the seat and turned to watch the trees and farmland streaming by the window.

CHAPTER FOUR

Rose emerged from her bedroom when they
returned, her hair mussed as if she'd been
napping, and joined Derek in putting groceries
away. Bobby and Kinsey fixed themselves gin
and tonics, and Bobby's frenetic energy finally
started to mellow.

That night Lars made spaghetti and baked
ready-made garlic bread. The group sat down
at the big table and dug in hungrily.

Rose broke the silence. "Something's
happening to me."

"What?" Marla asked through a mouthful
of pasta.

"Something's been . . . growing . . . in my head since we started this trip," Rose answered. "And today I finally figured it out." She took a deep breath and looked around importantly. "I've been hearing thoughts—your thoughts. I think it's astral projection. My brain is leaving my body and visiting your brains. Soon I'll have a full out-of-body experience." She stared solemnly at each one of them in turn.

Bobby's guffaw broke the silence. Marla elbowed him. "For once could you not so predictably be the asshole in the room?" she asked. "Just let her talk, okay?" She turned back to Rose. "What do you mean you've been hearing our thoughts?"

Rose smiled serenely. "At first I didn't understand what was happening, like when I felt that cop behind us on the way here. I thought I was making lucky guesses. But it's real. It's like people are talking inside my head, telling me what they're thinking."

"Bullshit," Kinsey said evenly. "That is such flaky bullshit."

"Really?" Rose said. "If I can't tell what you're thinking, then how do I know Bobby's ID got rejected at a restaurant today? How do I know he got in a fight? How do I know he's mad because he's almost out of coke?"

Kinsey's mouth opened. She struggled for words but couldn't come up with anything.

The rest of the group stared at her and Bobby, whose eyes were wide. "Well?" Lars asked, sounding skeptical. "Is she right?"

"What the fuck?" Kinsey asked. "What, did you bug the car or something?"

Bobby recovered sufficiently to say, "She probably just heard us talking about it."

"Well, okay," Diane said, her eyes gleaming with interest. "There's an easy way to prove this: Tell us what someone else is thinking. Something you couldn't know already."

Rose hesitated. "I'd feel bad . . . some things might be too private."

Diane thought for a moment. "Well, why don't we try to think of something we don't mind you saying, and you tell us what it is?"

"Okay," Rose said with a giggle. "I can't always hear everything everyone is thinking, so try to think of something random, and I'll see what I can pick up."

The table fell silent again, with everyone concentrating. Bobby and Kinsey pouted, exchanging glances with each other and shooting daggers at Rose.

"Well," Rose said, "Kinsey's thinking about throwing her wine glass at me."

"Lucky guess," Kinsey muttered, though she looked a bit startled.

Rose looked around the table, then settled on Diane. "You're picturing a . . . polar bear?" she asked.

Diane let out a little shriek, more delighted than scared. "That's right!" she exclaimed.

"You could've set that up before dinner," Kinsey said. "Doesn't mean anything."

"But we didn't!" Diane protested.

"That's okay," Rose said. "This is fun! Who cares what she thinks?" She looked around again and stopped at Lars. Her brow furrowed. "Slow down!" she said. She hesitated a moment more, then started saying haltingly, as if repeating someone else's words, "Eating other editors with each and every epileptic episode, elevated etiquette—" She broke off and laughed. "What the fuck are you thinking about?"

It was Lars's turn to look aghast. "It's a song. 'Alphabet Aerobics.' Blackalicious." He slumped backward, looking down at the table, shaking his head slightly. At last he looked up and grinned. "That's incredible. I don't know what the trick is, but it's fucking good. Is it lip reading? Were my lips moving?"

"It's not a trick," Rose protested, but Lars laughed and shook his head again. She looked at Bobby. "Come on," she said. "Play along. Think of something I couldn't know." Bobby glared at her for a few seconds. Rose recoiled a bit, then gave a forced laugh. "'Eat my shit you fucking cunt bitch?' Even I know I could have guessed that. Come on, try something a little more original!"

"This isn't working," Marla said. "We need outside verification." She got up and pulled at

Bobby's elbow. "Come with me and tell me something in another room where she can't possibly hear it. Come on, try to have some fun with us for once!"

Bobby scowled but finally relented. They went into the little room that served as an office and closed the door. The others looked at Rose expectantly, the food on their plates forgotten. When Marla and Bobby came back a few moments later, Marla looked somber and Bobby stricken.

"Did you get that?" she asked.

Rose shook her head, then stopped. "Wait." She froze, then looked down at the table. "Are you sure you're okay with me saying that?" She peered up at Bobby, whose expression was uncharacteristically serious.

"If you know what I'm thinking, might as well say it." He looked at Marla. "Sorry," he said. He sounded genuinely contrite. "It's the only thing I could think of that I'm sure nobody knows."

Marla looked ruefully at him and shrugged.

Diane couldn't contain herself. "Well? What is it?" she demanded.

Rose sucked in her breath, then slowly said, "Bobby had ancestors—great-great-great grandparents?—who had slaves."

"Whoa!" Lars said.

"Really?" Monique said.

Bobby looked mortified. He nodded. "Yeah," he said glumly. "My mom decided to do this genealogy thing last year. She found out then. It really fucked with my head when she told me. So messed up."

"Now does everyone believe me?" Rose asked.

"Yeah." Monique, her voice small and scared.

"I still think there's something else going on, but I don't know what it is," Lars said stubbornly, but his voice sounded less sure.

Rose sighed, a teacher impatient with a class of slow pupils. "Whatever. I don't need to convince anyone. This is my spiritual journey, not some party trick."

The group fell silent as their minds wrestled with what had happened. Derek broke the spell. "Well, Professor Xavier, what am I thinking now?"

"Um . . . you want me to help you with the dishes?" Rose ventured.

Derek smiled. "Exactly!"

Diane laughed uncertainly. Rose smiled at Derek and got up to help him clear the table. The others moved to the living room, where Lars started building a fire in the hearth.

"That was fucking crazy," Marla whispered.

Diane nodded, wide-eyed. "I know!" she hissed. "I still can't believe it."

Monique shook her head, her delicate features solemn. "No. It's crazy."

Lars said in a low voice, "I hate to admit it, but I can't figure out how she did that. I guess until I do, I can't totally rule out the possibility that she might have some kind of ESP." He shook his head. "Even saying it sounds ridiculous. But then again, she picked up on the exact part of the song I was thinking about, every word. It was incredible."

"I didn't believe in that shit either," Marla said. She shivered, and Diane pulled her close.

"So fucking creepy," Kinsey said. Bobby lay with his head in her lap, his eyes closed. Kinsey rubbed his temples with her fingertips. "Whatever she's doing, I hope it doesn't last long. If she's going to be telling everyone's secrets, shit is going to get awkward around here."

Lars nodded. "Yeah, it's . . . the possibilities are kind of scary." He looked toward the kitchen. Derek and Rose were side by side at the sink, washing and drying the dinner dishes. Their heads were close together, and they appeared to be deep in conversation. Lars wondered if she could hear their thoughts from that distance.

* * *

As soon as the others were out of earshot, Derek hissed to Rose, "Are you serious about this?"

She stared at him. "Didn't you see what I did? It's not a joke."

He scooped up empty plates and stacked silverware on top, then took the pile to the sink. She followed with several wine glasses.

"I'm worried about you," Derek said as he turned on the hot water and grabbed a scrub brush.

"I know," Rose said.

"Oh, what, are you reading my thoughts now?"

She nodded. "You don't even have to talk; it's like an echo when you do."

He looked closely at her. After a moment, her eyes widened. "You think this has something to do with what's going around school?"

He nodded.

"You overheard something," she murmured. "I can't . . . about this happening to the kids that left school and disappeared?"

He nodded again.

"So . . . you think I'm not really psychic now?"

"Actually, I do," he said aloud, though quietly. "I can't believe I'm saying it; I didn't think it was possible. But I'm worried about where you got it."

"Got it," she said softly. "So you think it's like a disease."

"Well . . ." he hesitated. "It is, I'm pretty sure."

She set a dry plate on top of another a little too hard with a loud clink. In a low, insistent voice, she said, "You don't know. If you knew how it felt, you wouldn't . . . it's not something that's wrong with me."

Derek searched for something to say, but Rose continued in an indignant hiss. "It's so right. And it's something I've wanted for so long! Something that proves there's more than just . . . this." She gestured with a dish, nearly dropping it. Her eyes grew shiny and wet with tears. "My whole life, I've been terrified of dying, ever since I was a little kid. I was so scared to think that my self, which feels so big and . . . necessary to the world, will just end someday."

"I know that, Rose, but—"

She cut him off. "But part of me still hoped there was an answer out there. There are so many forces we don't understand . . . I thought maybe there could be a chance that our energy is immortal. But I didn't really believe it, until now. This is just the beginning, I know it. It's the first step in becoming more. I'm not afraid anymore." She gulped back a lump in her throat. "For the first time since I can remember, I'm not afraid!" She looked at Derek. "You are, though." She hesitated. "You wish you hadn't brought me here."

Derek looked down. "No, that's not it. I just wish I'd gotten you here sooner. But I'm not going to let them find you. You'll get better soon."

"I don't want to get better," Rose muttered sullenly. They finished doing the dishes in silence.

* * *

Lying next to Monique in bed, reading, Lars started to nod off, his book dipping down to his chest before he jerked awake and started the process over again, eyelids slowly drooping.

Monique broke the silence, bringing him back from the brink of sleep. "I did know one of the girls who disappeared from school."

His eyes flared open. He looked at her, putting his book aside. "Who?"

"A girl named Jenny," she said. "I don't think you knew her. We had chemistry together. About a week or two ago, someone came and got her out of class, and she never came back. Derek didn't mention her; I don't think he knows she was one of them."

"How do you know? You don't know why she left school, right?"

"It has to be the same thing."

"But . . ." Lars searched for words. "But you said they came and got her. So she couldn't have been really sick, right? To be in school in the first place."

"Not sick the way you think of it," she said. "More sick the way . . . like my grandma was."

"Oh, Mo," he said and put his arm around her, squeezing her thin shoulders.

"You know?" she said. "Like, it was her mind that was sick. There was nothing wrong, like physically. But she changed, and after a while you could tell there was something really wrong with her. Then one day, someone took her away. It wasn't her parents. I don't know who it was. We all wondered about it for days, but no one ever found anything out."

"Why didn't you tell me?" Lars asked, bewildered. "Why didn't it get out to the rest of the school?"

"I don't know," Monique mused. "Now that I think about it, that's really weird." She lay quietly for a few moments. "It was the guy who came and got her. He didn't do anything bad, but he scared the living shit out of all of us. I guess I was afraid that if I said anything to anyone, he might find out and come back for me."

"Jesus Christ!" Lars said.

"Well, it was just kind of a feeling; I didn't actually think that. It was weird how quickly we all put it out of our heads."

Lars kissed her forehead again. "Is that why you didn't say anything about Jenny the other night?"

Monique nodded against him. Then he heard a sudden little sob. "And the other thing—" She swallowed audibly. "When Jenny first started acting different . . ."

Lars stayed silent and rubbed her back with his hand. She cleared her throat.

"She was always kind of a fuckup, you know?" she said finally. "She really didn't care about school. But then she started bragging that she was getting A's, and not just in our class. And she was doing it all without studying. She joked it was osmosis. But whatever, right?"

Monique shuddered. "Then she started doing this really annoying thing. She would stare at people and say what she thought they were thinking. Like if some guy was looking down a girl's shirt, she'd whisper, 'I so want to motorboat those.' Dumb stuff like that. Like, who couldn't guess that's what he was thinking? At first I just tried to ignore her, but then she did it to me. She looked at me and starting singing, 'Polly put the kettle on, we'll all have tea.' Toward the end, my grandma hummed that song all the fucking time. It still gets stuck in my head sometimes. But I know I wasn't humming it aloud. I was just thinking it. And Jenny, she looked at me and picked right up on it."

Lars's arm tensed and tightened around her. "Yeah," she said. "Just like Rose."

He finally spoke. "Did anything else happen before she . . . got taken away?"

"Yeah," Monique said again, reluctantly. "After a while, she started saying really weird, paranoid things. That's what reminded me of Grandma. One minute she's normal, the next she's accusing you of something. With Grandma, it was 'stealing her sweetheart.' Swear to God, she'd call me a whore to my face. Jenny was convinced someone put poison on her school supplies, and that our pens all had cameras in them. Then she started seeing things. She'd just stare past people at the walls, like she saw something moving. Once she screamed that someone was looking at her through the wall. I can't believe the teachers never did anything about it, but you know how it is. She'd always been kind of annoying, so it was easy to think all this stuff was just more of Jenny being Jenny.

"A day or so later, her mood totally changed. She was all happy and bouncy—a little too happy. It was creepy. That was when they came for her. She smiled at the guy and waved at everyone as she left. I don't think she even asked him where he was taking her, or why."

"That's it?" Lars said incredulously.

"Yeah. I don't know what happened to her after that. I don't think anybody ever found out."

He held her tighter. "Maybe nothing did. Or maybe she had a breakdown and now she's recovering somewhere. It doesn't mean anything bad is going to happen to Rose."

"Or us, if we catch what she has."

Lars frowned. "I find it hard to believe that whatever's happening to Rose is contagious."

Monique said, with some sarcasm, "I find it hard to believe what's happened to Rose, period. If that's possible, anything could be true."

The two lay quietly until they drifted off to sleep.

CHAPTER FIVE

"Jesus Christ, give it a rest!" Derek said with irritation.

Bobby and Kinsey looked up from the couch where they'd been making out more and more gratuitously, as the rest of the group tried to ignore them and focus on the movie that was playing. The two met one another's eyes, laughing a little breathlessly, and went upstairs.

Once in their room, Bobby pushed down on Kinsey's shoulders, urging her to her knees. Her breathing quickened even more as she worked at his belt. Bobby stood looking down at her, hands on the back of her head. As the sensations intensified, he closed his eyes and flung his head back.

Kinsey took a break to catch her breath, and he pulled her to her feet. They tore at their clothes, undressing as quickly as they could, and fell onto the bed together.

As Bobby plunged into her, his head filled with unfamiliar images and sensations. It was as if he were experiencing being Kinsey while looking down at her in real life. In his mind, his Kinsey-self was on her belly, being taken from behind, even though Kinsey was actually on her back. It was much more vivid than a fantasy; it felt real. A wave of nausea gripped his stomach as what he was seeing and what he was imagining progressed on separate tracks. Now in his imagination, his Kinsey-self felt sharp slaps from an open palm. This was accompanied by an actual moan from Kinsey.

In his mind, he-Kinsey turned to look over her shoulder at her lover.

Confused, Bobby watched through his Kinsey eyes to see a thirtysomething man with thinning hair behind her. With disgust, Bobby recognized Kinsey's crew coach, Mr. Whitney. His own revulsion grew even as his Kinsey-self's arousal increased.

"Wait!" Bobby said sharply, more to himself than to Kinsey. He pulled out of her and knelt on the bed, gripping the sides of his head. The image of Mr. Whitney dissolved; in its place was confusion—not his, but Kinsey's.

His eyes widened. He stared at her with dawning rage as she looked up at him, her chest still heaving. "What?" she said with a mixture of frustration and puzzlement. "Come on, let's keep going." She reached for him, and in Bobby's mind, the crew teacher reappeared as suddenly as he had disappeared, staring greedily at his Kinsey-self's body.

Bobby gave a cry of disgust and pushed Kinsey's hand away. She stared at him, startled.

"You—and him?" Bobby said in a guttural voice.

Kinsey's eyes widened even further. She stared at him, her mouth working as she tried to find words. "How did you—I mean—what do you—" Before she could string together a complete sentence, Bobby's fist drilled into her face, splitting open her lip and smashing her nose to the side.

Kinsey screamed and her hand flew to her nose. Instinctively she drew her legs to her chest and kicked as hard as she could. Her bare feet caught Bobby in the gut and propelled him backward. His flailing hands scrabbled at the bedcovers for a second but failed to find purchase. He slipped off the bed and onto the rough braided rug on the floor.

Kinsey caught a glimpse of herself in a mirror over the bedroom dresser, half obscured by a pile of crumpled clothes. Blood dripped from beneath her hand and she screamed again, more from pain and anger than from fear.

She jumped off the bed and onto Bobby, pinning his arms to the sides of his body with her strong thighs. She began slapping his chest and face wildly. He cried out as one of her fingernails scraped a red line from his earlobe to his nose. He managed to fling her off. She fell backward onto the hardwood floor with a loud thump.

Someone knocked at the bedroom door. "Guys?" Derek's muffled voice said, then Marla: "What's going on? Is everything okay?"

Bobby ignored them, his eyes locked on Kinsey. "You bitch!" he hissed. "You worthless fucking cunt! How could you? With a fucking teacher?" His voice broke and he started sobbing, a strangely childlike sound.

Derek flung the door open and rushed in, flipping the overhead light on as he did. The others stood outside the door and peered into the room. Diane gave a little shriek. Bobby and Kinsey were both bleeding now, although the thin streak of oozing red on his cheek paled in comparison to the blood dripping down the lower part of her face.

As she became aware of the group staring in, Kinsey grabbed her clothes from the floor. Bobby was still staring at her, his eyes now red and wet with tears. He sprang off the floor, seemingly unaware of his nudity, and went after her again.

This time, before his fist could reach her, Derek and Marla grabbed his elbows from behind. He struggled, and his shoulder caught Marla under the chin, smashing her teeth together. She fell back for a second, and Lars entered the fray. Together he and Derek pinned Bobby down and restrained his arms and legs.

"Dude, calm down!" Lars said. "What the fuck is going on?"

Bobby strained against both boys for a few more seconds then went limp, glaring over at where Kinsey stood, hands on her hips, her blood-smeared face defiant.

"That bitch cheated on me!" Bobby started to cry again. "With Mr. fucking Whitney!"

A chorus of voices expressed their disbelief. "Even if she did, that doesn't give you the right to hit her," Marla had the self-possession to say.

Derek struggled to get over his shock. "You guys have to stop. Look at you, you're both messed up. I don't want you to hurt each other anymore." He looked behind him. "Can someone get a washcloth or something?"

Monique broke away and went down the hall toward the bathroom. Kinsey moved toward the door, sidestepping Bobby pinned on the floor, and followed Monique. The others heard water running and the girls talking in low voices.

"All right, I'm done, let me go," Bobby said in a more resigned voice. "She's not fucking worth it." Lars and Derek released their hold, and Bobby stood. He looked at all of them. "Can you just go? I want to get some sleep." He grabbed a haphazard assortment of Kinsey's things and shoved them at Derek. "Take it. I don't ever want to see that slut again."

Derek took the bundle and moved quietly to the door, glancing at Bobby a few more times before leaving. Before he left, he whispered to Rose, "Let Kinsey know I'm putting her stuff in the room next to yours, okay?"

Rose, who had been staring off into space, shook her head slightly as she came back to reality. "Oh, sure," she said before wandering down the hall toward the bathroom. Derek watched her for a second, then went downstairs.

Lars put his arm around Marla's shoulders as they left Bobby's room. "You okay?" he asked. She nodded, moving her jaw gingerly. They went downstairs, Diane in tow. The three other girls stayed in the bathroom, talking quietly.

Downstairs, Derek prepared the sofabed in the office next to Rose's bedroom. He got himself a beer and took a long pull, his face drawn. Lars took three more beers from the fridge and brought them to Diane and Marla.

Derek added logs to the fire, which had been dwindling as they drowsily watched the movie. No one was sleepy anymore. Rose, Kinsey, and Monique came downstairs, and Monique went straight to the kitchen to make an ice pack for Kinsey's nose. Kinsey saw the drinks in everyone else's hands and said, "God, yes. Someone get me a beer."

Lars jumped up and retrieved one for her, then sat down heavily on the couch.

Monique brought Kinsey a dishcloth with ice cubes tied into it. As she handed it over she said softly, "Bobby's got the same thing as Rose."

Rose looked at her accusingly. "It's not the same thing at all," she said.

"But how did he know then?" Kinsey demanded. "About me and Rod." She shuddered. "Right when I was thinking about him, Bobby just suddenly knew. It was so fucking freaky." She sighed. "We started seeing each other about a month ago. I still love Bobby but Rod was just so much more, you know, adult. It was exciting." She touched her lip and winced. "But Rod's married; it's just for fun." She slumped down, and her face crumpled into tears.

Rose slipped away into her bedroom unnoticed. Monique whispered to Lars, "I want to go to bed. Come keep me company?" Her face was even paler than usual.

"Sure." He finished his beer in a couple of deep swigs and stood, helping her to her feet.

Marla looked kindly at Kinsey. "You going to be okay?"

Tears were still streaming down Kinsey's face as she held the ice pack to her nose, but she nodded. "Yeah, I'm fine," she said haltingly.

Lars and Monique headed upstairs, and Marla and Diane followed shortly after. Derek sat with Kinsey a while longer before they split up, Derek heading upstairs and Kinsey to her new room.

After everyone else was gone, Rose emerged from her bedroom. She knelt down in front of the slowly dying fire, staring at the embers. She stayed motionless for hours, long after the last hint of red had gone dark and cool.

CHAPTER SIX

Hector White stood in his office, staring contemplatively out the window. The view was of a bland parking lot surrounded by scrubby trees. Beyond the trees, he could just make out cows in a muddy field where the spring grass hadn't begun to grow in earnest yet.

Hector was thinking of the last time he'd seen Derek. The boy's frightened face and shaky voice, repeating directions and security codes Hector had forced him to memorize. Hector restraining himself from clinging to his son, giving him a quick hug instead. Watching the SUV as it turned a corner and disappeared.

A meeting notification chimed from his computer. Hector shook himself from his reverie and left his office. He walked down a nondescript hall of offices just like his, down to a conference room at the end.

He was the first one there, so he flipped on the fluorescent lights and sat down. He took his phone from his pocket, checking his personal email out of habit. He felt both relief and worry when he saw there were no new messages from his son. He'd told Derek not to contact him or use any trackable communications devices. Now he was in the unfortunate situation of not knowing whether his son was obeying his directions, or if something had happened to Derek that prevented him from contacting his father.

Hector ran his hand through his short salt-and-pepper hair. Decades of learning to control his emotions kept him outwardly calm as he recalled, with horrifying clarity, the day he learned that a subject from the Petri Dish had infiltrated his son's school.

It was an idiotic oversight. Their contact in the Petri Dish, posing as a secretary, was meant to monitor requests for transfers into and out of the small high school. But a messy divorce led to a sudden move, the mother gaining conditional admission into a new school before she'd formally transferred her child out of the other one. Due to inefficient paperwork processing between the two districts, weeks passed before his organization realized what had happened.

By then, it had spread to several teens in his son's high school. Even in Petri Dish it had spread much more quickly and easily than expected. The catastrophic failure of the experiment was evident, and the operation had turned its focus to quarantining the infected in both schools and suppressing the potentially explosive story before it reached any credible news outlets.

That's when Hector gave Derek the keys to the Suburban, a wad of cash, a credit card linked to Hector only through a false identity, and verbal instructions (nothing in writing) on how to get to his lodge, also deeded under another identity.

John Kitterly, Hector's supervisor, came into the conference room looking harried. Three others followed shortly.

"All right, let's get started," Kitterly said. "Mary, what do we have?"

The steel-haired woman adjusted her glasses and opened a folder. "Containment in the Petri Dish and the surrounding municipality continues. So far we've had three attempts to contact the media with a story contradicting our official position, all successfully discredited. Five missing-persons reports, which we've gotten escalated to the FBI and out of the local PD's jurisdiction."

"And what about our recruits?"

The woman's lips pursed almost imperceptibly. "So far ninety-six have responded to TD 554. Of those, forty-seven have progressed past final stage mission failure. The remaining forty-nine are under observation. They were all later recipients, so we expect they too will experience failure."

Kitterly shook his head. "And . . . Petri Dish Two?" He gave Hector a sidelong glance.

A heavyset, balding man to Mary's left spoke. "As you know, Petri Dish Two suspended operations a week ago. Since then, surveillance has been extremely difficult. We have operatives gathering email, phone, and other activity and sifting through it. From intel gathered thus far, we estimate forty-five recruits. Considering the population of Petri Dish Two is six times that of the first school, this is astounding. If our records are correct, the closure has at least been extraordinarily effective at containing the experiment."

Kitterly sighed. "Some good news at last."

"Since Two is in a far more affluent and suburban area, we expect there to be more difficulty suppressing panic and far more missing-persons reports and attempts to garner media attention. However, thus far only eleven recruits have succumbed to mission failure, and this was only within the last week or so.

Right now, our primary action item is to monitor all the subjects' movements. In light of the closure, there's greater danger of subjects leaving town and potentially passing the experiment on, creating more petri dishes. So far, most have stayed close to home. We've alerted all schools in the area to a confidential report about a particularly virulent strain of influenza causing Petri Dish Two's temporary closure. We've warned them not to accept any transfers from the school, to prevent any parents trying to enroll subjects elsewhere.

"There are twelve subjects unaccounted for. It's unknown whether they responded to TD 554. We're tracking their families' communications and movements and expect to locate all of them." He took a deep breath. "We can only hope they don't spread it anywhere else."

"All right," Kitterly said. "Anything else?"

Mary spoke up. "For all that's gone wrong, one big win is that the organism's effect shows absolutely no ability to spread beyond the target age group. No one younger than fifteen or older than eighteen has shown any response to it."

"Thank God for that," Kitterly said heavily. "Any other good news?"

Mary and Charles shook their heads. The last man at the table spoke up. "At this point, we should just be glad none of us are attached to the initial decision-making of this program. If we keep managing to this level, we can probably expect a commendation. And if we come across a subject who doesn't progress to failure, we'll receive partial credit for that too." He smiled grimly. "All things considered, our role has been largely positive." He glanced at Hector, then down at the table.

Kitterly nodded. "Agreed. We'll reconvene this time tomorrow unless any irregularities surface before then." He stood. "Hector, I'll walk you back to your office."

Hector and Kitterly walked down the hall in near silence. Once they were in Hector's office and the door was closed, Kitterly got to the point. "Hector, you know I'm damn sorry this got so close to your family. You've been a real champ through all of it." He hesitated. "As you know, surveillance is standard for all households containing a possible recruit. I hate to pry, but . . ." He cleared his throat. "I requested a list of the unaccounted for, and your son is on it. I'm guessing this is due to whatever countersurveillance measures you have in place at home. So I'll just ask you straight: Are you in control of your son, and does he show any signs of responding to TD 554?"

Hector's face was impassive. "Absolutely. He's at home. He hasn't made contact with any of his . . . fellow subjects since the school closed, and he's shown no symptoms."

Kitterly looked at him for a beat, then clapped him on the shoulder. "I'm real pleased to hear that, Hector. I'll have Charles take him off his search list and mark him as contained and unresponsive. You just let me know if his status changes." He headed toward the door, then turned. "As you know, the lab guys are working around the clock to develop a cure. You have my personal assurance that if anything happens to Derek, we'll make sure he receives the best care possible."

Hector reached out to shake Kitterly's hand. "I appreciate that, John. I'm just glad I can take some work off of Charles's plate. As far as I'm concerned, with Derek safe, this is just a mission like any other. So you can take off the kid gloves." He managed a grin, and Kitterly chuckled with relief.

Once his supervisor had gone, Hector went back to his window. He pulled out his phone and checked for messages again. Nothing.

* * *

"Derek, have you seen Rose?" Marla asked as she helped him haul wood from the shed.

"Not for the last day or so," he said. "Well, not face to face. But I knocked on her door last night before I went to bed. She told me to leave her alone." He laughed humorlessly. "Not exactly reassuring, but at least she's alive and can talk."

"I don't know what's happening," Marla said. "At first I thought she was just pissed because none of us are happy about her weird psychic thing. But now I'm afraid it's something else."

"I know," Derek said, "I'm worried too. But she'll let us know if something is really wrong."

Back in the house, they stacked the wood next to the fireplace. Lars was washing dishes with his headphones on. Monique and Kinsey, who had grown somewhat companionable since the night of Bobby's meltdown, were painting each other's nails. Diane was deep in a book, but she looked up and gave Marla and Derek a little smile as they came in.

Marla went over to her and bent down for a kiss. She whispered, "Any sign of Bobby or Rose yet?"

Diane shook her head. As far as she knew, Bobby was still in his room. Rose had been gone when everyone else got up that morning. Her bedroom door had been ajar, so several of them had poked their heads in to make sure she really wasn't there.

"Want to go for a walk?" Marla asked Diane. "See if we can find her?"

Diane put her book down and nodded. "If we could at least talk to her and find out why she's been acting this way, I might not worry as much."

Diane put on her coat and hat, and the girls walked out. They'd gotten into the pattern of following the same route they'd taken the first day at the lodge, and occasionally Rose had joined them.

They walked up the hill, across the open flat area, and into the narrow stand of trees. They held hands as they strolled. "I kind of feel like we've been here forever," said Diane.

"I know," Marla said. "It's hard to imagine life at home anymore, but things are kind of getting crazy. I don't know how long we can last here, you know?"

Diane murmured agreement. "I do like spending all my time with you, though," she said with a little smile. "Seems like a good sign for us living together someday, huh?"

Marla squeezed her hand and kissed her. They lingered in the moment, closing their eyes. When Diane opened her eyes, she realized the stone ruins were in sight. She pointed.

Rose sat cross-legged on one of the larger rocks, holding a notebook and pen. Her unkempt hair drooped down on either side of her downturned face.

Diane hung back for a second, but slowly followed Marla as she approached the rock.

When they got a few yards away, one of them stepped on a twig that snapped with a sudden sharp sound. Rose looked up, the quick movement of her head like that of a spooked deer sensing a hunter.

"Hi, Rose," Marla said. They walked closer to her.

Rose put her hand over what she'd been writing. "Why are you here?" she asked. "Did they send you to report back?"

"Who? Derek?" Diane asked.

Rose laughed. "Derek, right," she said. "He's not really in charge. I'm talking about *them*."

Marla spoke reassuringly. "No one sent us, Rose. We just hadn't seen you in a while and missed you. We wanted to see if you were feeling okay."

Rose studied them. "How do I know you're not in on it?" she asked.

"In on what?" Marla said. "I don't exactly know what you're talking about, but whatever it is, can't you just read our minds and see we're not?"

Rose hesitated. "Yeah, yes, I can still do that." Her shoulders relaxed a bit. "All right, so maybe you're innocent bystanders. Come here. I'll show you what I've got so far."

She held out her notebook so that they could both see it. Indecipherable sketches and scribbles filled the page. She flipped backward, and they could see her scrawls covered most of the earlier pages as well.

"See, I thought, there has to be a reason they brought me here. Finally I figured it out."

She pointed to what could be a drawing of the lodge and surrounding hills. "It's easier for the satellite to home in, see? The waves just kind of fall down the hills onto us. Much more effective than if we were on level ground or on a hill." She looked up, her eyes darting left and right. "Which is why I've been up here so much. Making it harder for them."

"To do what?" Diane asked, bewildered.

"Scan off my brain," Rose said impatiently. "The satellite scans off parts of it, kind of like peeling layers of an onion. They've been after it since they figured out I was getting to a higher level of consciousness, and now they're trying to harvest that power for themselves."

"Who are 'they'?" Marla asked, trying not to sound too incredulous.

"I don't know yet," Rose said. "That's the last piece of the puzzle." She looked kindly at the girls. "Listen, I'm glad there are at least a few people who aren't in on it. But I think I can make more progress on my own, you know?"

Marla and Diane glanced at each other. "Sure, Rose, we'll leave you alone, for now. But come home before it gets dark, OK?"

Rose gave them a little smile but didn't answer.

They returned to the lodge and told Derek about Rose's state of mind. He looked worried, but when Diane asked if he thought Rose should go home, he grew evasive.

"Let me talk to her when she comes home. You know she's always been a little melodramatic. I bet I can calm her down."

"Derek, it was really scary," Diane said. "I've known her a long time too, and I've never seen anything like this."

"Just give me some time," he said. "Okay?"

"Okay," Marla said after a pause.

"Okay," Diane said, more reluctantly.

The three of them stayed up late, later than even Bobby, who was still drinking and smoking more than usual. By two o'clock in the morning, when Rose still hadn't appeared, Marla looked at Derek in appeal. "What are we going to do?"

He was hunched and tense. "Don't know." He thought. "Can you show me where you saw her last? Maybe she's still there and we can talk her into coming back with us." They got their coats on. Derek found a flashlight and they left.

As they approached the ruins, they saw nothing at first. Then a flash of pale skin came into view. Derek trained the flashlight on Rose, curled up asleep on the ground.

Marla crouched close to her and shook her shoulder. Rose stirred and blinked in the glare of the flashlight, and Marla waved Derek away frantically. He stepped back and pointed the beam elsewhere.

"Rose," Marla whispered, "come back to the house."

Rose sat up and rubbed her eyes, then nodded. The knowing gleam in her eye seemed to be gone. She let Marla help her up and lead her back the way they'd come.

She seemed unusually jumpy, starting several times at sounds and shadows as they walked through the woods. But they got her into her bed without incident. Derek and the girls collapsed in their own beds, exhausted.

Less than two hours later, the entire house echoed with screams.

CHAPTER SEVEN

On the second floor, lights came on and doors opened. The screams came again from downstairs, and everyone bolted toward the sound.

Downstairs, they heard Kinsey's voice, husky with sleep. "What's wrong?" She came out of her room as the others reached the main floor and went to Rose's door. Marla knocked, then opened the door and stepped in without waiting for a response.

It took a moment for her eyes to adjust to the dark. When they did, she saw Rose crouched in the corner of the room. Marla hurried to her.

"Careful!" Rose said in a choked voice.

Marla spun around, saw nothing, and turned back to Rose. "What is it?" she said, her own voice shaking.

"That . . . thing!" Rose said, pointing with a trembling finger at the wall next to the door. Marla looked again. She stepped to the door and flipped the light switch.

"There's nothing to be afraid of in here, Rose," Marla said. "See?"

Rose looked at Marla, then back at the wall. "N-nothing?" she asked tremulously.

"That's right," Marla said. She helped Rose to her feet for the second time that night and led her from the bedroom. Rose looked around at the rest of the group in a daze.

Derek held his hand out to her. "Rose, if you don't want to go back in there, you can come sleep in my room."

She hesitated at first, but eventually crept toward him. He put his arm around her and led her upstairs. Everyone else soon dispersed to their rooms as well.

Upstairs, Derek turned off the overhead light but, at Rose's plea, left a bedside lamp on. He helped Rose get in bed, then climbed in beside her. They lay in silence for several minutes until Rose spoke.

"There was something awful in my room," she whispered. "I don't know what. Scales and teeth and eyes."

He pulled her closer. "It was just a dream." Eventually they drifted off into an uneasy slumber.

* * *

Rose laid down the last card in her hand. "I win!"

Everyone stared.

The group was gathered in the living room the next evening, playing games and watching a movie. Bobby and Kinsey were speaking for the first time since their fight, even cautiously flirting. Other than an air of concern over Rose's condition, the mood was light.

Rose had consented to a card game with Diane and Marla. At first she only half seemed to be paying attention. By the time she laid down her final card with a triumphant cry, her mood had been utterly transformed. A bouncy song came on in the movie, and she leapt to her feet dancing, spinning in a circle and laughing.

Her friends exchanged glances as they watched her. She stretched out her hands to Diane and Marla.

"Oh no," Marla said with a smile. "I don't dance. Especially not in front of anyone."

Rose shrugged and beckoned to Diane. When shaking her head didn't dissuade Rose she obliged, bashfully shuffling her feet to the beat.

Rose turned to the rest of the group. "Who else?" she asked. "Come on, dance party!"

With a puzzled smile, Derek stood and took her hands, leading her through a sloppy little swing dance move.

Lars stayed seated next to Monique, who wore a cloudy expression. But Bobby and Kinsey joined in, smiling at each other.

Rose twirled around the living space, occasionally bumping furniture and stumbling. Each time she did, she laughed more. It delighted most of the others, but Monique shook her head. "No, no, no," she moaned.

Lars put his arm around her. "Is this what happened to Jenny?" he whispered. She nodded miserably as she watched the dancers.

At last, Derek plopped down next to her, smiling and panting a little. "What do you think's gotten into Rose?"

Monique hesitated, then leaned over to whisper in his ear. As he listened, he grew pale. Lars leaned in too, and the three of them spoke in low tones that the music and laughter from the others masked.

Lars beckoned Marla over. Soon Diane noticed and came over as well. Besides Rose, only Bobby and Kinsey were still dancing, locked in a sinuous rhythm, oblivious to the solemn discussion on the couch. Soon they went upstairs to the room they'd shared until their fight, leaving Rose to leap and spin around the room with hectic merriment.

The others watched her. At last she swayed gaily over to join them. "What's up?" she asked.

Derek turned off the movie. He looked at the floor in the sudden quiet. Monique was the first to speak. "We think . . . there's something really wrong with you," she said.

Rose laughed loudly. "Oh, you guys," she said. "You've been saying that for ages, and now that I'm feeling better than ever, you still think so?"

Derek said softly, "Your mood changed so suddenly. We're worried it's part of what's happening to you."

Rose rolled her eyes in mock exasperation, still smiling. "What will convince you I'm fine?"

Lars spoke up hesitantly. "We just have to wait it out," he said.

"What?" Rose said, still swaying to the music.

"Well, we don't know if anything else will happen to you. If it doesn't, maybe we're wrong."

"Great!" Rose said brightly. She twirled away, then came back. "Is that it? We just wait?"

Lars glanced at all of them again, then continued. "We don't want to worry about you running off or something else bad happening . . ." he began.

She bobbed her head. "So what?"

"So . . . we think we should . . . restrain you for the night," he said.

"What's that mean?" she said. "God, spit it out already!"

"We . . ." he took a deep breath. "We want to tie you to your bed to make sure you're still here when we wake up."

"Ooh," she giggled. "Kinky! Well okay, if it'll make you happy."

Somehow her reaction made it even harder, but Derek went rummaging through the house until he found a length of rope. He cut off four pieces and ushered Rose into her bedroom. She lay down, still smiling at him, and let him draw one hand at a time up to the slatted headboard. He tied the knots as best he could, then did the same with Rose's ankles.

"Are you okay?" Derek asked when they were finished. "Are you comfortable enough?"

Rose wiggled her hands and feet slightly and smiled blissfully. "I feel amazing," she said.

Derek put a thick comforter over her and pulled it up to her chin. "I'm sorry," he said. "We're just trying to keep you safe."

"It's okay," Rose said sunnily. "I love all of you for caring so much, but I'm going to be fine. You'll see."

* * *

The next morning, Derek awoke before anyone else. He went downstairs and started a pot of coffee. He went to Rose's door and listened for any sign of movement. When he heard nothing, he fixed himself a bowl of cereal and sat down with a book.

The others emerged sporadically from upstairs. By ten thirty even Bobby and Kinsey were awake, looking happier than they had in days. But there was still no sound from Rose's room.

"Do you think she got out?" Diane finally said.

As Marla filled Kinsey and Bobby in on what had happened after they'd gone to bed the night before, Derek knocked on her door, lightly at first and then harder. When there was no response, he turned the knob as quietly as possible. Everyone else lowered their voices to murmurs as he eased the door open.

The curtains were drawn and the room was dim, but he could see her on the bed. There was something too still about her. He moved closer.

Heart in his mouth, he flipped the light switch.

CHAPTER EIGHT

In the living room, the others heard Derek's cry of horror. He came out as they reached the door, his face pale, almost greenish. He slumped against the doorframe. "There's something . . . wrong." The others looked in.

Rose lay still under the comforter—or rather, her body did. Dried blood obscured most of her hands and face. Blood had soaked through the comforter that covered her, then dried in large brownish patches.

Lars moved forward, but Derek lunged in front of him. "Don't get near her!"

"But we have to help her!" Lars said.

"We can't," Derek said quietly. "Look at her. She's gone."

"Well, we should still try to see what happened to her."

"I know what happened," Derek said. "It's that thing that's going around school."

"What have we done?" Diane sobbed. "What are we going to tell her family?" Marla led her from the room and sat her on a couch, holding and rocking her.

"We have to get to town so we can call someone," Marla said. "Her family, an ambulance, the cops?"

"No!" Derek came out of the room. His face was still sickly pale, but his voice was firm. "We can't."

"What?" Marla said. "But we have to. We need to get help, we need to let people know what happened. We can't just stay here with a—" She gulped. "A dead body, acting like nothing's wrong." Her voice quavered, but she held herself together and stroked Diane's hair.

Derek said, "We need to think—oh god, Rose." He stopped for a second to catch his breath. "This thing—if anyone finds out—"

"We didn't do anything wrong," Lars said, still staring at the bloody bed. "We have nothing to hide. The ropes—we can explain we were scared she might leave. We can explain everything."

"No, I mean . . ." Derek went back into the room and pushed everyone out, then shut the door on the horrific sight. "Listen to me," he said. "It's not just a disease. The others were taken away. If whoever took them away finds out we were with someone who died from this thing, we'll all get taken."

The others gaped at him. At last, Marla found her voice. "But even if that's true, what's the alternative? How are we going to deal with Rose? And what if we do all get . . . what she had? Maybe the ones taking people away are doctors or scientists. That may be our best chance to stay alive."

Derek shook his head. "They don't have a cure. And if we didn't catch it, if we're okay, they might still get us if we tell anyone."

"You're thinking about dumping her body somewhere," Bobby mused. Derek narrowed his eyes at him, and Bobby bit his lip. "I mean, that must be what you mean."

Derek looked at him a moment longer, than slowly nodded. "Yeah," he said. "Get rid of her body. Take it somewhere it can be found, where no one would know she was with us." He ran his hand over his face. "Poor Rose. But we couldn't have done anything to help her. She had this thing before we left home. Now we have to try to save ourselves. Maybe the rest of us will be okay." He looked around at everyone. "Don't you see what I mean?"

Monique burst into tears and pressed her head against Lars's chest. Marla looked confused and uncomprehending as she held a still-sobbing Diane, but Bobby and Kinsey were nodding slowly. "What should we do with her?" Bobby said.

Derek paced back and forth, shaking. "I don't know, I don't know," he muttered. "Her mom . . . I don't want her to just disappear and not have her family know."

"Okay," Bobby said. "We can't go home yet, right? This thing is still happening there."

Derek nodded. "I think so," he said. "I'm pretty sure it was just beginning when we left."

"So we need to drop her near home without being seen," Bobby said. "At least over the state line, in Virginia somewhere. Tonight, after dark."

"Wait!" Marla said. "Do you fucking hear yourselves? This is so crazy."

Derek looked at her. "I'm not going home," he said. "Not now."

Her eyes were wide. "Let's just think about this, Derek. We don't want to do something insane that we can't take back."

"Marla's right," said Lars, wiping his eyes. "This is huge. We need to come to an agreement before we do anything."

Derek looked as if he was going to protest, but Bobby said, "Okay, we can wait until tomorrow. It doesn't make any difference."

Kinsey shuddered. "I can't stay in a house with her," she said. "We have to do something today. Can't we just run away?" She shook her head. "No, we can't. I'm going to college in the fall. We need to figure out how to save ourselves."

Bobby said, "I think we should stay here until we calm down. Derek, you help me put . . . the body somewhere else."

Derek nodded slowly. He turned to the others. "You might not want to see this."

While the rest huddled in the living room, Derek and Bobby went to the shed and came back with a tarp, a knife, and some work gloves. Derek had also found disposable facemasks, which they put on. They put the tarp on the floor by the bed and cut the ties that held Rose's corpse to the bedframe. Derek tucked the edges of the comforter around her, then stood at the foot of the bed while Bobby went to the head. Together, with grunting effort, they rolled the body off the bed and onto the tarp. They heard horrified gasps from the main room when Rose's body made an audible thump on the floor. They themselves could hardly suppress their emotions when they saw how the blood had soaked into the sheets. Peeling them back, they saw the mattress was stained as well.

"We can burn this later," Derek said to Bobby with grim calm. He pulled a spare blanket from the bedroom closet and covered the blood-drenched bed.

Then he and Bobby folded the tarp around the stiff body. Together they lifted it and staggered out of the bedroom. They avoided looking at their friends as they made their way toward the door. Kinsey ran to open it for them.

When they got to the shed, the door was still ajar, as they'd left it. Bobby nudged it farther open with his shoulder. The air inside the long, narrow space was as chilly as the air outside. When they laid the body in a corner of the room, Derek lost the composure he'd managed to maintain through the ordeal. He burst into rasping sobs. Even Bobby had tears in his eyes.

"Hey, we're doing the right thing, man," he said, putting his arm around Derek. "Let's go." Derek threw both arms around Bobby and buried his face in his neck. Bobby stood and let him cry for a while, awkwardly patting his back. He kissed the top of Derek's head. "Let's go," he said again, more gently.

They walked back to the front of the house. Inside, the air was thick with sorrow.

The day passed agonizingly slowly; at the same time, the shadows of dusk seemed to come from nowhere. When it came time to sleep, Kinsey went with Bobby to the upstairs room again. There was no mention of her sleeping in the room next to Rose's.

* * *

At some point in the night, Monique arose and left the room she shared with Lars. He didn't stir.

* * *

The silence of the lodge was once again shattered by screams. Exhausted minds swam into consciousness and bedroom doors were flung open. In the hallway, Derek, Lars, Marla, Diane, and Bobby looked at each other with tired, fearful eyes. Kinsey and Monique weren't there.

Another scream snapped them into action, and they raced down the hall to the bathroom door.

As they crowded to peer inside the small room, Kinsey moaned. Not Monique. Monique lay still and silent in the bathtub. Only her neck and head were completely visible in the murky reddish water. Her drawn face looked older and even paler than usual. Without the red lipstick she wore every day, her lips were thin and colorless.

Kinsey stood beside the tub, her hands clamped over her mouth. Her eyes were wide, and she didn't make another sound.

Lars pushed past the others and stumbled to the bathtub. Kinsey moved out of his way.

"No, no," he moaned quietly. He knelt on the tile floor and stretched out a hesitant hand to touch Monique's cheek. He shrank back at the feel of it at first, then touched it again, then reached into the bloody water and grabbed her shoulders. He tried to shake her, though she was so stiff she didn't move much. "No, no, no!" he cried. He laid his face on top of her head and began to sob.

Kinsey held tightly to Bobby. "I just came in here to pee and there she was. I didn't know what to do. I couldn't hear her at all. She wasn't . . . thinking anything." She shuddered and pressed her face into his chest. "That's how I knew she was dead."

Derek finally pried himself from the doorway and went in. "Lars . . ." he said gently. He put his hand on the other boy's shoulder.

Lars shook as if to move his hand. "Just leave me alone, please," he said in a muffled voice.

Derek nodded. "Okay, man." He left the bathroom and closed the door so it was only slightly ajar.

Moving down the hallway with the air of a sleepwalker, he paused at the door of the room Lars and Monique had shared and looked in. He saw it almost right away: a couple pieces of paper folded together and stuck into the frame of the mirror above the dresser. He hesitated, then plucked the papers from the mirror.

"Should we . . . let Lars read it first?" Diane asked in a small, tremulous voice from the doorway.

Derek thought for a moment before shaking his head and unfolding the note. "I don't think Lars can handle anything else right now." He held the papers with shaking hands and read silently with Diane looking over his shoulder. When they were done, he passed it around so they could all read it.

To Lars (and everyone),

I'm so sorry. I know I have it too. I
started hearing your thoughts a couple
days ago and hid it because I wasn't
sure what to do. Then I saw how Rose
died and knew what was waiting for
me.

I went to look at her body in the shed
tonight. I wasn't scared of being infected
because I knew I already had it. I
wanted to see how bad it was. Pretty
fucking bad. There were little bloody
dots all over her, like she'd been pricked
with pins thousands of times. I see that
every time I close my eyes now.

I don't that to happen to me, and I don't
want to lose my mind first. The way
Rose acted near the end, it was so much
like my grandma's dementia. I don't
want to spend my last days like that. I
want to go while I still feel like myself.

Please, if you see my parents again, tell them I love them and I'm so sorry this happened. But tell them I would've died anyway; I just chose the way to go.

Derek: Don't feel bad. You tried to save us. You couldn't help that we were already sick before we came here.

Lars, I love you. You're the best friend I ever had. If you don't get what I have, I hope you get out of this and live a happy life.

Bye, everyone. If you believe in anything bigger than us, pray for me.
Monique

* * *

Somehow it fell to Marla to bring the letter to Lars, who was still in the bathroom. He was slouched next to the tub. Some of the reddish water had slopped onto the floor.

Marla hesitated in the doorway. "Lars," she said softly.

Lars turned at the sound of her voice. "Hi, Marla," he said dully.

She pushed the note at him. It took a while for his hands to respond, but eventually he took it from her. He started to read it and his sobs started again, though with less energy.

Marla crouched next to him. "Do you want me to leave?" she asked.

He started to nod, then said, "No, wait. Could you stay?"

She sat on the floor with her back against the wall while he finished reading.

When he finished, he looked at her. "Why couldn't she talk to me?"

Marla hugged her knees to her chest and swallowed. "I guess . . . she knew you would stop her."

"Fucking right I would have!" he said. His voice broke off in a choked sob. "What are we going to do now?"

"I don't know," Marla whispered. Then she straightened her shoulders. "You should get some rest. Derek will figure out what to do, and I'll help him."

"I'll stay in here," Lars said, but his voice and his eyes were heavy and dull.

Marla got to her feet with some effort; she too was nearing the end of her strength. She offered him her hand. "Come on," she said. He looked into her pinched face, and she managed a little smile. At last he took her hand and stood.

No one was in the hallway; the others must have been downstairs. She led him to her and Diane's room. "You might sleep better in a new room," she said. Lars's mouth tightened into a grimace as another wave of sadness broke over him, but he slumped onto the bed without resistance. Marla covered him with a blanket and leaned down to kiss his cheek. His eyelids started to lower; he was already well on his way to sleep when she closed the door.

Marla went downstairs and joined the other four, who were sitting in shocked silence in the living room. Diane came to her and held her tight.

Marla stroked her back. She looked at Derek. "We have to do something, don't we? With Monique?"

"We shouldn't leave her in the water," he agreed.

"So we still don't think we should call anyone?" Diane asked in a plaintive tone.

Derek shook his head. "We'll still have the same problem we did before. When they saw Rose's body, they would know we were around someone with the disease. We need to try to hide the bodies or leave them somewhere where they'll be found. We still need to protect ourselves." He started to stand, then collapsed back onto the couch. "I'm just not sure I can do it again."

Marla extricated herself from Diane's arms. "I'll do it," she said. She pressed her lips together to stop them from quivering. "But I'll need help." She looked at Bobby with raised eyebrows.

He nodded. "Are you sure you can do it though?" Bobby asked. "It's a lot harder than you'd think. The . . . other one . . . was really heavy."

Marla smiled grimly. "I know I look scrawny, but I can do it." She turned to the door resolutely. "Let's get this over with."

She and Bobby retrieved rubber gloves and another tarp from the shed and brought them upstairs into the bathroom. "We should let the water out first," Marla said, then shuddered. "I really don't want to reach into all that blood. We don't know how it's transmitted."

Bobby didn't look at her. "I'll do it," he said. He put on a pair of the rubber gloves and reached into the tub. He grimaced as the murky water slopped against his bare arm, but he managed to find the plug and pull it out.

As the water drained, Monique's body slowly came into view. Both Bobby and Marla tried not to, but they couldn't stop looking at the pale puckered skin, pinkish from the residue of bloody water, and the thin, lifeless limbs.

They spread the tarp next to the bathtub. Marla put her gloves on and steeled herself for what was next. She placed her hands under Monique's arms while Bobby gripped under the knees. He nodded to Marla, and the two strained and lifted the body. Their grasp slipped a few times, but eventually they lifted Monique out and onto the tarp.

"Should we try to get her dressed?" Marla asked. "It seems terrible to put her out in the cold like this."

"Sure," Bobby said. With much effort, they pulled on Monique's pajamas over her wet skin, gingerly avoiding the deep red cuts on her inner wrists. The clothing looked twisted and ill-fitting, but at least she was covered.

They both stood in silence for a moment, looking down. Marla's mind flooded with disbelief about how macabre it was to dress a corpse that had once been their acquaintance.

"I know," Bobby said.

Marla was too exhausted to react. Instead, she crouched again and started wrapping the body in the tarp.

Getting Monique through the bathroom door and to the top of the stairs was the easy part. They struggled down the steps with Bobby going first, bearing most of the weight. The body kept threatening to slip out of Marla's arms, but she managed to hold on.

Derek, Diane, and Kinsey watched them from the living room area. As Marla struggled once more and nearly dropped her end of the wrapped corpse, Diane leaped up. Though she was crying, she managed to help the pair lift their burden and carry it toward the door.

In a moment of déjà vu, Kinsey held the door open. The three made their way out and around to the shed. When they got inside, they hesitated.

"Where?" Marla grunted.

"I guess next to Rose," Bobby said. They lowered the body as gently as possible next to the other tarp-covered shape.

"Let's get out of here," Marla said. They backed out hastily, shut the door, and made their way back inside.

* * *

The group, now smaller with Rose and Monique gone and Lars sleeping upstairs, sat mutely in the living room.

Eventually Diane said, "We need to talk to Lars before he finds her gone." The others nodded solemnly.

"Let's wait until he wakes up," Marla said.

"I want to watch something stupid," Kinsey said. "I can't think anymore." She went to the cabinet and pulled out a DVD. No one argued, so she put it on. They sat in a daze through the entire thing, gradually sinking into numbness under the burden of their grief and horror.

When it was over, Marla and Diane murmured goodnight and headed upstairs.

It wasn't until they got to their door that Marla remembered she'd put Lars in their bed. She turned to Diane, put a finger to her lips, and slowly turned the doorknob.

Inside, Lars stirred and turned over. He sat up as they crept into the room. Marla turned on a bedside lamp. Lars looked at them with tired, uncomprehending eyes until the realization of what had happened resurfaced.

He buried his face in his hands and moaned. His shoulders shook as he started crying again.

Marla and Diane sat on either side and hugged him, feeling the sobs wracking his body, tears welling up in their own eyes.

He took his hands from his face and wrapped his arms around the girls, and the three of them rocked together, crying, for several minutes. Then Diane kissed his cheek impulsively. He turned to reciprocate, and his mouth landed on her lips instead. They hesitated, then kissed fiercely, their tears mixing on their cheeks.

CHAPTER NINE

Marla lifted her head off Lars's shoulder, her
eyes wide as she watched them kiss. Lars
turned to her, looking shocked himself.
Hesitantly, he put his hand on Marla's cheek
and kissed her too. Marla gasped and closed
her eyes as she responded.

They kissed some more then lay down
together. Marla and Diane pressed their bodies
against Lars. His breathing quickened. Marla
touched his warm, flat belly, then moved her
hand down, slipping under the loose
waistband of his jeans and under the snugger
fit of his underwear.

Piece by piece, clothing began to come off. Their bodies intertwined, feeling hot skin and beating hearts magnified by three.

The girls worked their lips down Lars's chest and belly. He moaned softly, overwhelmed. Diane moved back up to kiss Lars's lips. He pulled her farther up so he could reach her breasts with his mouth.

Diane practically saw stars; waves of arousal coursed through her body. She moved her hips as his hand started stroking her. She grew still and quiet, lost in the sensations until, gasping, she collapsed against him.

Lars guided Marla her onto her back, then moved his head down between her legs. She gripped the headboard and arched her back. Diane kissed her, and she responded urgently, her moans muffled against Diane's lips.

Lars moved back up to lie between them again, and the girls stroked him and kissed his cheeks and neck. He pulled them closer, gripping their waists. "I want you both," he whispered tentatively. It the first time any of them had spoken.

Marla and Diane nodded against his chest. "Really?" he said with disbelief in his voice. When they said yes, he knelt above Diane and eased his way into her. They moved slowly and softly together for a few minutes before he kissed her and moved over to Marla.

Diane lay back a bit and watched them, drinking in their bodies joined together. Despite how surreal it all felt, her hands crept to touch herself until Lars met her eyes and climbed on top of her again.

Lars went back to Marla, and shortly he started a different rhythm that led him to climax. He collapsed onto the mattress. They were quiet in the dark except for their breathing, slowly returning to normal.

"I'm sorry," Lars murmured at last. "I don't know what . . . I mean, I know you're . . ."

Diane shushed him, Marla pulled the sheet and comforter up from where they'd puddled at the foot of the bed, and the three of them curled up close under the blankets.

They lay in silence again. Diane found herself wondering how Lars had known just how to pleasure them both, tailoring his touches and movements to accommodate their particular desires.

Then she heard, as if Lars was whispering in her mind, "I don't know. It just came to me. Like your bodies were telling me what to do."

Marla thought, and they both heard, "Am I hearing what you're thinking?"

Feeling the shock of the other two as well as their own, they reeled with the realization simultaneously.

"Is this really happening?" Diane said silently. She sensed affirmation from both of them. Somehow she was certain they were understanding and answering her.

"This is incredible," Lars thought. "This whole night has been." He squeezed the girls, and they both leaned in so he could kiss them, one after the other. "Especially after . . ." His mind, and consequently theirs, suddenly flooded with images of Monique, the reddish water, her pale lips. His hold on them slackened as horror rushed over him.

"Monique . . . how could I be happy so soon after she . . ."

"None of us meant for this to happen," Marla thought. "But it felt so right, like it was meant to be."

"Oh my god," Diane thought suddenly. "This means we have it, doesn't it?" Her icy fear coursed through the other two. "This means we're all going to die soon."

They huddled together, feeling one another's scattered, frightened thoughts as clearly as they'd felt their hands and mouths exploring each other's bodies. Eventually exhaustion overtook fear and the girls dropped off into a fitful sleep.

Lars, who had slept for the entire day, stayed awake, feeling their thoughts drain away until he was left with only his own, and an occasional nonsensical burst of dream imagery from them. He eased his arms from under the two girls and rolled onto his side. He stared at Marla's thin, dark shoulders and felt Diane inch closer to him in her sleep. His senses were overwrought with pleasure and excitement on one hand, and the dark horror of the past couple of days on the other. His eyes filled with tears. He reached his arm around Marla and tugged her close. Being pressed between the two girls was unfamiliar, but at the same time it felt like the only good thing in the world.

* * *

Late the next morning they awoke, almost simultaneously, to the sensation of their bodies pressed together. Under normal circumstances they would have been self-consciously remembering about what had happened the night before, twisting themselves in knots as they wondered what the others were thinking. But instead, they could sense one another's feelings and know that everything was fine.

Lars, wide awake despite his mostly sleepless night, kissed each of them deeply, then quickly pulled his clothes on. By wordless agreement, they decided to keep what had happened a secret from the others. He cracked the door and peered into the hallway to make sure no one else was awake, then went to his room.

To all of their surprise, they could still read each other as clearly as when they'd been in the same room. The girls' hearts ached when Lars saw all of Monique's things and felt a huge pang of loss. They felt as guilty as he had the night before for enjoying themselves so soon after her death.

Lars reassured them with his thoughts. Then he had a vivid flashback to the night before that made both girls' faces grow hot.

Lars thought about taking a shower but then remembered what had happened in the bathroom. Marla realized with a guilty start that she and Bobby hadn't returned to clean the room after taking Monique out of it. Instead they took turns using the downstairs shower.

By the time they were all done, the others were stirring. They could read everyone's thoughts, though not as clearly and completely as one another's. They could immediately tell everyone was in a bad way, especially Bobby. His thoughts came in short, incoherent bursts.

"It's like how Rose was a few nights before she died," Diane thought worriedly. Then, "I wonder if anyone else can hear our thoughts?" But she didn't sense any reciprocal recognition coming from any of their friends' minds.

Diane wandered into the kitchen to make a batch of French toast, but they were nearly out of staples. She settled on a bowl of dry Cheerios, scooping them up with her hand to eat them. Marla came in and sat next to her, then Lars appeared, his hair damp. They looked bashfully away from one another, but images from the night before flashed back and forth between their minds. Lars started to come toward them, drawn irresistibly, but heard footsteps on the stairs and stopped in his tracks.

Derek appeared. He too was carrying a towel. "Hi," he said. He looked calm, but his mind was like a rat's maze he kept scurrying around, looking for a way out. He headed into the bathroom and started the shower.

Soon after, Kinsey came down. She looked haunted, with dark puffy circles under her eyes. She nodded at them, distracted. "Is there any coffee?" she asked.

"I'll make some," Diane said. She went to the cupboard.

"What the fuck?" Kinsey said suddenly. "Seriously?" They all sensed her surprise as she got glimpses of what they'd done the night before. The three of them were taken aback as well; only Marla had realized that Kinsey had developed the same powers a couple days before then, and in the chaos of everything else, it had slipped her mind. The fact that no one had seemed to notice their thoughts while upstairs had increased their sense of security about keeping their secret. Either Kinsey had been too sleepy before or her powers weren't strong enough to read thoughts of people in other rooms, Marla thought.

"You can read people's thoughts from a different room?" Kinsey said aloud. "Jesus Christ, I can't. How long have you had it?"

"Just started last night," Lars said.

"Well I've had it for days, ever since Bobby and I got back together, and I've never been able to hear anything unless I'm right near somebody." Her mind wandered to Bobby as she said that and they could feel the fear growing in her. They tried to ascertain what was wrong but her thoughts about him were scattered and hard to read.

"How—how is—" Diane struggled for a casual way to ask it while she got the coffee brewing, but before she could come out with a complete question, they heard his feet on the stairs and she clammed up.

As Bobby got far enough downstairs to become visible to them, they could feel each other's mutual shock. His face looked haggard; probably the result of over a week of hard drinking and smoking and the stressful events of the last couple days, but somehow it seemed to have happened to him overnight. The previous couple of days he'd seemed relatively even-keeled, considering the circumstances, and more helpful and empathetic than he'd ever been. Now he looked haunted, suspicious, and angry. His hair was unkempt and his wrinkled clothing looked like it had been pulled from a dirty laundry pile. They'd never seen Bobby not look pulled together.

"What are you looking at?" he snarled at no one in particular. The others made a concerted effort to turn their eyes elsewhere.

Just then, Derek emerged from the bathroom, wearing only a towel and a shocked expression. "So you all have it now?"

They all turned to look at him.

"I . . . guess so," Lars admitted. "Do you?"

Derek shook his head slowly. The trio and Kinsey all felt his fear radiating off him, and the single overriding thought he was having: "I've got to get away from them."

"Hey, wait," Lars protested. "You can't just leave us stranded. If you take the car, we won't have any way of getting out of here ourselves."

Derek looked at his friend with a combination of sorrow and disgust. "Leaving here isn't going to save any of you," he said. And he thought, "And I don't want you infecting anyone else, especially me."

"Fuck that!" Kinsey said. "We need to get help—look at Bobby! You need to tell us everything you know about this thing so we can figure out who can help us. I don't want to die!"

Derek looked around, then at the door. Bobby raced to it and stood with his back against it. Kinsey stood at the foot of the stairs so he couldn't go up to get dressed. "I know you know more than you told us!" she said furiously. "I know your dad is in on it. Now tell us the whole fucking truth!"

Derek stood in his towel for a moment. Then he ducked back into the bathroom and put on his pajamas from the night before while the others waited. "Okay," he said as he re-emerged. "Fine. Everything I know."

CHAPTER TEN

Derek sat on one of the sofas. Marla and Lars sat too, but Bobby and Kinsey stayed in their positions protecting the exits.

Diane brought cups of coffee to everyone. Derek hesitated and looked at the mug before accepting it, and she heard in his mind that he was wondering how the disease was transmitted. "Do I have to even say anything?" he asked with a touch of sarcasm as he watched her face. "Can't I just think it and you'll read my mind?"

"No!" Kinsey said. "I want to make sure I get the whole thing. But don't even try to hide anything; these three can read every single thing everyone thinks."

Derek started haltingly. "My dad—he always just said he worked in the government, you know? He never talked much about his job. I guess I never really thought about that. Well, sometimes when people would talk about their parents' jobs, I would kind of think 'Hey, they know a lot about that. How come I don't?' But then I'd ask my dad and he'd give me some boring explanation—managing information systems, implementing programs—and I'd just kind of tune out because I didn't understand anything he was saying.

"But around the time this weird stuff started happening at school, he started acting funny. A couple of times I caught him shouting at people on the phone. Once I heard him say, 'That's my son's school!' I felt too scared to ask him about it, I guess. I just eavesdropped as much as I could. I figured out there was some kind of test thing that they were doing in some other school, and somehow one of the kids had come over to ours.

"The day after they closed our school, I said something about having friends over. He yelled at me that I couldn't. When I asked him why, he just went into his office and shut the door. But around dinnertime, he came out and told me I needed to get out of town as soon as possible.

"I asked him why and he finally told me some of what he knew. I'm sure it wasn't the whole story. But he said the organization he worked for had been doing an experiment at a school in the middle of nowhere to try to develop, like, psychic powers in the students. They have a kind of synthetic virus that could—I don't know, I didn't understand most of it—but anyway, they fixed it so it could only pass among teenagers. They didn't want it to spread to young kids who might not be able to handle it, and they didn't want adults to get it because they might be too hard to control once they became psychic." He let out a grim half-laugh. "Yeah. He said that.

"So they thought it was ready to test in the real world, and they put it in this school. He didn't tell me how it spreads. Really wish I knew that." He eyed them each in turn. "But the thing failed. All the other stuff that happened after the ESP, the stuff that happened to Rose, that wasn't supposed to be part of the experiment. They wanted people alive so they could figure out how to use their powers for, like, spying or whatever. They didn't expect anyone to die.

"And then this girl transferred to our school. She brought it with her. My dad was so mad because it wasn't ever supposed to spread.

"So he told me to get away. He told me not to bring anyone with me, to just get out, and hopefully I wouldn't have caught it. He said to call him if I thought I was getting the symptoms and he'd try to come help me. Otherwise, he said, just stay here and wait for him to contact me or come get me." He laughed bitterly. "And I haven't gotten it, not yet anyway. But shit, I wish I'd listened to him about not bringing anyone."

He put the untouched coffee down on the table next to him and leaned forward. "Listen guys. I brought you with me, I broke my promise to my dad, because you're my favorite people. I wanted to protect you. But it came with us. Now I'm the only one who doesn't seem to be sick, so I'm the only one with a chance of saving myself. Can you just let me? I'll explain everything to my dad; he'll make sure everybody's—everybody gets back to their families somehow."

Before anyone else could decide how to respond, Kinsey yelled, "No!" They all looked at her. "There has to be a way to get better. Your dad's job made this thing—great! Take us to him and tell him we need help."

Derek struggled to find words, so the trio read his thoughts with horror before he was able to articulate them. "Listen to me. They don't have a cure. They're just trying to round up the kids that have it. If you live, they'll keep you and study you, try to make you do things for them. If you die, you're just a specimen for them to dissect and experiment on."

Diane started to cry. Lars and Marla moved to either side of her to comfort her. Lars took her hand and kissed it. Surprise registered in Derek's expression and mind, though he didn't say anything.

Lars spoke up, his voice rough with emotion. "If that's how it is, I guess I'd like to stay here. If I only have a week or so left before things start going haywire in my head, I want to spend it being as happy as I can be." Diane cried harder but nodded. Marla reached over and squeezed Lars's hand.

"Well, not me," Kinsey said. "I'm not happy here, and I'd rather take a chance with the evil government." Her voice got husky. "I'd also like to see my family and other friends; I never said good-bye. I didn't know we'd be here so long."

"That's true," Diane said, her voice shaking too. "Thinking about my mom and dad worrying, never knowing what happened to me . . ."

"But there's one more thing we have to think about," Lars said, looking at Derek. "Isn't there?" Derek nodded grimly, and Lars went on, although the others could read his and Derek's thoughts clearly. "We could all be carriers of this thing. If we leave the lodge and come in contact with any other people our age, even by accident—we don't know how it's transmitted. We don't know how to protect them. We could start some kind of epidemic." He looked at the girls. "Could we live with that?"

"But that's true for Derek too," Kinsey said accusingly. "You've been around all of us this whole time. Even though you're not showing symptoms now, that doesn't mean you couldn't pass it on to other people."

He stood up. "But I've got a chance. I'll be careful until I get to my dad. He'll make sure I'm okay before I get around other people my age again." He shivered. "The longer I stay here, the more chance that I might still get it, if I don't have it."

A guttural sound came from Bobby, and everyone turned. They'd forgotten he was standing by the door; he'd barely moved or made a sound.

"This. Is. Such. Bullshit!" he growled. "Don't you see? Don't you all see? It's him! He brought us all here to experiment on us. And now that it's done, he wants to leave us to die!" He stalked over to Derek. "I know you have a cure. Some kind of vaccine you took so you wouldn't catch it. You better give it to us. You better fucking give it to us."

Derek tried to stay outwardly calm though his mind transmitted his fear clearly. "Bobby, that's not true. I was trying to save you all. I would still try to save you if I knew a way. I didn't know this would happen."

"Give us the cure!" Bobby stabbed his finger into Derek's chest.

Kinsey came over and tried to grab Bobby's arm, but he shook her off. "Baby, this isn't real," she said. "What you're thinking, it's part of the sickness. That's why I want to get you home to see if we can get you help. You've gotten worse. You can't even read my thoughts like you could before, huh?"

"Yes I can. I can read everything he's thinking. He's the agent. It's him!"

The other four sensed only bewilderment in Derek's mind at the accusation. Lars approached Bobby. "Hey," he said. "Let's take a step back and think about this, okay man?" He put his hand on Bobby's arm.

Bobby turned to him, nostrils flared, and threw a punch. Lars saw it coming and flinched, which probably saved a few teeth or bones from being broken when Bobby's fist made contact, but he stumbled backward and sat heavily on the floor. His nose and lip were bleeding and he seemed stunned, though not badly hurt. Marla rushed to him and examined the injuries. Diane hurried to the kitchen for a cloth.

A sudden shriek from Kinsey got their attention. Bobby had Derek pinned to the floor, hands around his neck. Derek struggled to speak. "Don't do this—I love you."

"Bullshit!" Bobby yelled and increased the pressure on Derek's neck.

Kinsey screamed again. "Stop it! He's telling the truth! You know that, Bobby. You heard him think it."

"It was lies!" Bobby said through gritted teeth. He began to shake Derek, his hands still squeezing his neck. "They put that there, in his brain, to fool us. Just part of the big . . . fucking . . . experiment." He lifted Derek's head and smashed it down again to punctuate the last few words. It hit the stone area in front of the fireplace with three sickening thuds.

Marla and Kinsey grabbed Bobby and tried to pull him off Derek, but his vicelike grip was nearly impossible to break. By the time they pried his fingers off, Derek was limp and still, his face dull. His head lolled lifelessly back onto the blood-stained stones.

CHAPTER ELEVEN

Marla knelt over Derek's body. She shook him gently by the shoulders, then put her head on his chest. She called his name with increasing urgency, but he was unresponsive.

Bobby stood up and backed away. He raced to the door and ran outside.

Kinsey looked between the door and the group surrounding Derek's body, momentarily frozen. Then she too rushed out the door. They heard her calling Bobby's name, her voice—and her thoughts—growing fainter.

The trio stared at Derek's body, too overwhelmed with panic to feel grief.

"Oh, this is bad, this is really bad," Marla said in a low voice. "We have to get away now or we're going to get blamed," she added silently.

"What about Kinsey?" Lars thought. "We can't leave her here."

"We don't even know where either of them went," Marla countered. "How long should we wait? Should we go look for them?"

"Shit," Lars thought suddenly, "I'm not even sure where the keys to the car are. We can't leave anyway unless we find them."

They began searching likely spots: the row of hooks by the door, kitchen drawers, Derek's coat. Marla searched Derek's room. Lars went outside and made sure they weren't in the ignition of the Suburban.

They were still looking twenty minutes later when they heard the door to the lodge open. Everyone froze. Lars peered in from the main-floor bathroom where he'd been searching.

He relaxed. "It's Kinsey," he broadcast to the girls. They came downstairs.

"What happened? Did you find him?" Marla asked.

Kinsey shook her head. "I saw him going that way—" she gestured to the front of the house "—up that hill and into the woods. I followed him a little ways, but I worried I was going to get lost. Or—" she stopped talking, but the others clearly followed her thought process: She was also afraid of what Bobby might do if he decided she was part of the conspiracy he'd made up.

"We've been looking all over for the car keys, but haven't been able to find them," Diane said. "Do you know where they are?"

Kinsey shook her head, looking worried. "I hope you weren't planning to ditch us."

"No, we were going to wait 'til you came back," Marla said, trying not to think about how that hadn't really been decided yet. "But now that you're here, we should talk about what to do." She glanced at Derek's body. Kinsey followed her gaze and paled. Marla continued. "Bobby did that. Rose and Monique dying, that wasn't any of our faults. But—" her voice caught and she waited a second to recover. "Now this. And they'll think we had something to do with it. I think we should try to get away."

"You mean go home?" Kinsey asked.

Marla hesitated. "I don't know . . . if we go home this might come back to haunt us. I think we should go somewhere, be different people if we can. I know it sounds crazy but . . . I don't see how we're going to get our old lives back." Her voice choked up again. "Things have changed forever now."

"But we can't leave Bobby out here all alone!" Kinsey spluttered. "It wasn't his fault, you know. It was this disease. Temporary insanity or whatever. And if we don't go home, there's no chance to get help. We'll all just die in a few days anyway."

"And possibly spread this to other people," Lars spoke up, heavily.

The four sank into a dispirited silence.

"Well," Marla said slowly, "I guess we should wait and try to see if Bobby comes back. We don't want to leave you here, Kinsey, and you wouldn't leave without him. We don't know where the keys are anyway, so we can't leave even if we wanted to."

"Can we, um—" Kinsey eyed Derek. Diane sighed in a way that sounded like a sob.

"He tried to save us, and now he's dead because of it," she said.

This time Kinsey and Lars took the body out. Since there was far less bleeding, and they knew they were already infected, they didn't take as many precautions. They simply picked up Derek's body and hauled him out to the back shed. Neither of them had been in it since the bodies of Rose and Monique had been moved here. They instinctively recoiled at their first glimpse of the corpses wrapped in tarps in the corner and left Derek just inside, uncovered, to the right of the door.

They stepped out and Lars collapsed into a crouch on the ground, holding his head in his hands. He didn't sob audibly, but his shoulders shook. Kinsey bent over awkwardly and patted his shoulder.

He could feel Marla and Diane worriedly questioning him in his mind. After a while, he stood up, wiped his face with both hands, scrubbed his eyes with the heels of his hands, and they went back around to the house.

Back inside, Lars and Kinsey slumped on chairs in the living room. "Maybe we should just try to get out of here," Kinsey said hoarsely. "Even if we find Bobby, what if he's totally gone crazy and we can't get him to come with us? And then if we get him help, he's going to be arrested for killing Derek." She started crying, loud plaintive sobs. "I can't figure out how to help my baby. I don't want to leave him, but what else can I do?"

"Well," Diane said glumly, "We can't find the car keys anyway, so how are we going to get out of here? Walk?"

"That's a thought," Lars mused. "It's about ten miles to the nearest town; we could make it. And maybe we could . . . we could use our phones to find a bus or train station or something."

"What about hot-wiring the car?" Kinsey said suddenly. "We should at least try that before we give up on it. We'd be able to get so much farther without having to see anyone, so you know, less witnesses."

"I guess," Marla said dubiously. "Does anyone know how to, though?"

Kinsey stood up. "I mean, I've heard something about it. Seen a couple movies where it happened. I think we need to unscrew the thing around the ignition, or break it open somehow. I'll see if I can find a screwdriver or something." She left the lodge hurriedly, glad to have something to do.

While she was gone, the trio split up again to search for the keys. "This is so crazy," Diane thought. "No matter what we do, there's nothing we can do to change things."

"We have to try, sweetheart," Marla cast back at her.

"What about passing it to other people?" Diane wondered.

"We'll just have to be really careful," Lars thought.

Kinsey came back in with a toolbox. "Found some stuff," she said.

The four of them went out to the Suburban and Lars opened the driver side door. He crawled through to the other side of the seats to make room for Kinsey. She set the toolbox on the ground, opened it, and took out a screwdriver. "Let's see what I can do," she said with doubt in her voice. Marla and Diane peered in as she started to work on the driving shaft.

None of them heard the thoughts of another person nearby, or felt his eyes watching them from the hill.

CHAPTER TWELVE

Dressed in camouflage, Hector felt confident the teens would never notice him. His heart was cold and his head clear.

It hadn't been when he'd first peered into the shed behind the house and confirmed what he'd thought he'd seen Lars and Kinsey doing.

His journey to West Virginia had started the day before, at work. It was seven in the morning when Charles came to his office; they both tended to start work earlier than their other colleagues. "Hector, I know you're fully booked right now, but I could really use someone to bounce ideas off of."

"Sure," Hector said, gesturing for Charles to take a seat in a chair in front of his desk.

Charles pulled out a piece of paper, frowned at it. "It's the missing subjects from Petri Two. Seems like I've been spinning my wheels for the last couple of days. I've located four of the missing dozen. One other was—" he cleared his throat uncomfortably "—your son, and you vouched for his whereabouts, so he's off the list. But there are seven more, and we don't have any leads. Their parents haven't filed missing persons reports, so we assume they think their kids are okay, but there's been no contact in days. We got some information from wiretaps, but all the leads we followed up on turned out to be dead ends. One said she was visiting her cousin in Southern Virginia. That cousin has been located and the subject isn't with her. It's been the same for all of them. None of the things they've told their parents have checked out. Two of them took out quite a bit of money before they disappeared. They both used the ATM the same day."

He pushed the list across Hector's desk to him. "You're good at thinking outside the box. Maybe you can help me think of more creative ways to look for these last seven." He looked at Hector, who seemed to be frozen, staring at the paper. "You okay, Hector?" he asked.

Hector recovered quickly and looked up from the paper as if it meant nothing. He rattled off a few ideas of ways to look for the subjects, but his mind was reeling. The list was burned into his mind. Monique Severson. Lars Michaels. Marla Rudd. Diane Thornton. Bobby Stevens. Kinsey Cheatham. Rose Martin. Every single one made frequent appearances in Derek's social media, had been to the house, came up often when his son informed him of his plans. Derek didn't know every student in the high school, even though he was popular. What were the odds the seven missing kids all just happened to be connected to Derek?

He gave a few more suggestions he knew Charles would have already thought of, and Charles sighed. "Well, thanks anyway, Hector. Hell, at least I know I've been following up on everything that you would have. I guess I'll just have to keep watching their houses, emails, social, and hope for some kind of clue that way." He stood and picked up his list. "Let me know if you get any other ideas."

Hector agreed and showed him calmly to the door. Then he went to his favorite spot by the window. His heart and mind were both racing. "That stupid fucking kid," he thought, but he felt a little pride. His son had tried to save more than just himself; he'd rounded up his friends, and been smart enough to have them all create different cover stories so they couldn't be traced together. It was the only reasonable explanation.

He had to see if his theory was correct, and make sure they were okay. He feigned a headache and left work. He went home, but only briefly. He changed into camouflage, collected some supplies and weapons, and headed out of town.

The trip was shorter and much less eventful than that of the teens. He drove to a little dead-end drive between trees a half mile from the lodge and left the car, strapping a holster with a handgun to his chest. He put on a backpack containing ammo and other supplies. Then he traveled on foot across the familiar landscape in a beeline toward his lodge.

As he came to the top of one of the hills surrounding the place, he dropped to a crouch and got closer, moving from boulder to bush. He pulled binoculars from his backpack and surveyed the area. From his vantage point, he could see both the front porch and the shed in back.

Just then, a boy ran from the house. Hector thought he recognized Bobby. The young man was moving erratically, looking fearfully around as if he was being followed. Hector watched, frowning, as he ran across the lawn and began frantically clambering up a steep hill nearly opposite the one Hector occupied.

A few minutes later, a young woman with an athletic build ran out as well, long blond hair streaming behind her. She seemed to catch sight of the young man and climbed up after him, but he soon disappeared from view. The girl lost his trail and wandered aimlessly across the hill, weaving in and out of clusters of trees.

So at least two of Derek's friends were with him. Hector wondered if Bobby's behavior might indicate that he'd caught TD 554. Icy fear gripped Hector's heart. What if Derek had already succumbed to it? But he realized that seeing Bobby run away might not indicate anything. Maybe it was a game. Maybe he'd fought with his girlfriend. Any number of things might have caused his uphill sprint.

Hector inched closer. He found a boulder about halfway down the hill surrounded and overgrown by tall weeds. He hunkered down and continued to survey the lodge and surrounding area through his binoculars. Nothing was visibly amiss; his Suburban was parked outside, and it and the lodge looked as they always did.

Another young man emerged from the house. Lars, Hector thought. He peered into the driver's side window of the SUV before returning to the lodge. After a while, the girl came back down the hill. Hector scrutinized her face and confirmed it was Kinsey. She went into the house.

There was no more activity for a few more minutes. Then the door opened again. Hector focused his binoculars on it to see who came through it.

It was Lars, carrying something with effort. Hector's stomach clenched with dread. It was the feet of a lifeless body. Kinsey appeared, holding the upper part of the body under its shoulders.

The two teens struggled down the steps and started around the house. Hector focused in desperately on the face of the corpse. He nearly dropped his binoculars from numb fingers, cursed, and regained his grip. He put them back up to his eyes, hoping he would see something other than what was coming into focus. Hoping the slumped, inert body was anyone else but Derek.

Of course it was Derek. His darling son, the only person in the world that he considered family.

Despite Hector's sickening horror, he kept still and watched as the teens reemerged from the shed. He felt a stirring of pity despite himself as the boy fell to his knees and Kinsey attempted to comfort him. Then the two went around to the front of the house and went inside.

Hector began to move forward, slowly but purposefully, keeping his motions limited and stopping frequently whenever he came to a spot that would conceal him from the house. He didn't know when someone else might be coming out.

He reached the bottom of the hill, crossed a tiny creek with one bound, and hid behind the trunk of a large pine tree for a moment. Then he hurried to the shed, the door of which was ajar, and slipped inside.

He saw his son almost immediately, lying on the filthy floor. Hector's heart dropped into his stomach.

He knelt and examined Derek's body, feeling his wrist in vain for a pulse. There was none of the stippling of skin nor the vast quantities of blood associated with TD 554 failure. He noticed a shadow on Derek's neck and looked closer. Fresh bruises, clearly made by fingers. He lifted his son's head tenderly and noticed the still-drying blood on the back of his head, and felt where Derek's skull had cracked.

Hector paused, his head down, eyes closed. No tears came. The sharp searing pain he'd felt at first ebbed away. With the acceptance his son was dead came a cold, emotionless calm. He thought with pleasant anticipation of storming into the lodge and killing Lars, Kinsey, and anyone else who was still alive, and then hunting Bobby through the familiar land around his lodge.

But he dismissed the idea just as quickly. Now that Derek was gone, he found his main priority had once again become his employer.

He stood up and surveyed the shed—and that's when he caught sight of the lumpy tarps pushed into a corner.

He unwrapped one body and noted its slashed wrists without emotion. Inside the

second tarp he saw an all too familiar sight—
the crusted blood and ghastly symmetrical
pinpoint sores that TD 554 had left on many
young victims.

He carefully rewrapped the bodies and
tried to make them look exactly like they had
when he'd first encountered them. Just then, he
heard footsteps approaching the shed. He
crouched behind several large metal containers
and stilled his breathing—and his thoughts, as
he'd been trained to do, in case whoever was
coming was a TD 554 recruit.

The shed door opened and someone came
inside. They rummaged around, but near the
other side of the long narrow room. Hector
peered out cautiously and caught sight of a
flash of long blond hair. Kinsey.

She picked up a toolbox and started to turn,
so he ducked down again. She left the shed,
slamming the door shut behind her.

Hector crept out of the shed as soon as her
footsteps faded and made his way back to his
vantage point halfway up the hill. Just as he
settled in and lifted his binoculars again, four

teens came out of the house, Kinsey and Lars plus two more girls, one short and pale with short brown curly hair, the other dark-skinned and nearly as tall as Kinsey.

He watched them open the door to the SUV, and he saw Kinsey pull a screwdriver from the toolbox. She settled behind the wheel of the car and started fiddling with the ignition. He smiled. Clearly they were trying to start the car without the keys. Which meant they didn't have the keys. He knew the antitheft mechanism would lock down if they actually succeeded in opening the drive shaft up.

He stole back up the hill without a glance back and hurried through the same countryside the way he'd come, back to his car. Then he drove toward the nearest town.

He checked his phone periodically, and as soon as he saw he had reception, he pulled over. He dialed a number, waited, and spoke into the phone. "Charles?" he said. "I've found your missing Petri Two subjects. All of them. And I need backup to help retrieve them." He hesitated. "I'll explain everything later."

* * *

Kinsey's screwdriver slipped again. She swore and slumped back on the seat, sulking.

"Can I give it a try?" asked Lars. Just as he was about to take the screwdriver, he paused. They all felt a wordless chaos growing in their minds. Someone's thoughts, but barely human.

Suddenly Diane screamed as she fell against the SUV where she'd been standing outside watching Kinsey.

Bobby had come out of nowhere and slammed into her. "Think you can leave without me?" he said between gritted teeth as he pummeled Diane. His movements were wild and uncoordinated, but he still managed to punch her in the stomach.

Marla shoved Bobby with all her might. He flopped backward onto the ground and lay for a second, stunned, then leaped to his feet again.

Marla opened the driver side door and jumped in, shoving Kinsey over toward the passenger side, and hauled the stunned Diane in after her with a strength born of desperation.

She reached past Diane and pulled the door shut, then slammed the lock down. All the doors locked with a click.

Bobby pounded on the driver's side window, and Diane, who was practically pressed against it, screamed again. He jumped onto the hood and slapped both hands against the front window, making a feral growling sound. The car's occupants recoiled, pressing back against the seats as far as they could go.

Bobby snarled and jumped off the car on the other side, banging the window on the passenger door. He pulled his arm back and punched the window, making a sickening thud with his fist, blood splattering onto the glass from the split skin of his knuckles. He backed off and shook his hand but didn't seem to be fully aware of how much it should have hurt him. He ran to a pile of firewood by the porch and grabbed a thick stick off the top. He ran back to the car and started circling it, pounding at the windows at random. He didn't cause any visible damage but the vehicle's occupants clung to each other, frozen, overwhelmed by the barrage of noise.

Bobby drew back a few feet on the driver side, like a bull getting ready to charge, fumbling in the pocket of his coat as if searching for a weapon. His body tensed and they braced themselves for the onslaught.

Instead, Bobby froze, looked comically surprised, and dropped to the ground as a loud flat report rang through the air.

CHAPTER THIRTEEN

"What was that?" Kinsey shrieked. The four looked around wildly to try to figure out what had just happened. Bobby was on the ground, stunned, twitching.

Marla pointed with a shaking hand. The others saw it at the same time. Two people, a man and a woman, striding toward them. They were wielding rifles.

They could hear the man, a lanky, scrawny man with tinted glasses and a grease-stained baseball cap. "Think they got guns?"

"These pussy bitches? Hell no," the woman said. She had a frizz of hair carelessly clipped back from her face. Her features looked too small and delicate for her large face.

"Oh my god," Kinsey muttered under her breath.

"What?" the others asked simultaneously. Then, all at the same time, they received vivid images from Kinsey's head. The diner. The tired waitress with the square face. Bobby posturing, threatening. The skinny kid coming between him and the waitress, who Bobby had known was his mother. Bobby shoving him against her.

The waitress. Sherry. That was definitely her outside the car, though her face looked colder, angrier, and something else—

"She's on something," Lars thought. "Ice, I bet."

The man next to her wasn't her son, Kinsey thought—couldn't be. He was shorter and looked older, with more facial hair than the skinny kid could have grown since the last time she'd seen him. She watched the man shift a lump of chew from one side of his lip to the other and spit.

The couple approached the car. Sherry peered in at them, her eyes red and glassy. She looked past Marla and Diane and quickly settled on Kinsey. "That's the one, baby," she said, jerking her rifle toward her. "She was with that diseased sack of shit."

The man cocked his rifle with a practiced motion and a loud, ominous crack. "All right," he said, raising his voice to make sure the kids could hear him through the windows. "Y'all get out of there now."

Diane clung to Marla. Kinsey and Lars were frozen in place. None of them could formulate any sort of response.

The man's tone was calm, even easygoing, though his voice was muffled behind gritted teeth. "Y'all get out so's we can talk to you, or we'll just shoot you right now." When they still didn't move, he unhesitatingly fired into the front windshield with a deafening sound.

The bullet didn't go through the glass; it ricocheted off. But the glass partially splintered in a spiral that radiated out from where it had been struck.

"Next one's gonna get through to ya," the man said in a chillingly casual tone. "Y'all got one more chance to get outta there now." He cocked his rifle again.

"All right!" Marla shouted, finally finding her voice. "Don't shoot." More quietly, she said, "Come on guys, let's go. We have no chance in here."

She reached across Diane and opened the driver side door. Diane cringed away from the opening, toward Marla, but Marla calmly forced her out. Lars and Kinsey slowly got out on the other side.

While the man stepped back and kept his gun at the ready, Sherry came toward the passenger side and pointed her gun straight at Kinsey. "You," she said flatly. "Y'all get over here."

Sniveling, seemingly riveted by the barrel of the rifle, Kinsey moved toward the woman. "I didn't do anything to your son," she said.

"Oh, you a little mind reader too?" Sherry said almost cheerily. "Well, you sure as shit was part of it."

Marla, Diane, and Lars read the woman's mind with horror as she remembered everything that had happened over the past week or two. Her son, suddenly acting strangely, insisting he knew what everyone was thinking. Claiming he'd passed a kid in the grocery store who was thinking about a virus that caused psychic powers, worrying about his friends, one of whom was the guy who had shoved her son in the diner that day. Her son, seemingly more and more able to read her thoughts every day, until one day he devolved into incoherent paranoia. Sherry turning to her boyfriend's meth pipe to dull her fear. Her only son, now hallucinating monsters in every corner. Her grief and rage, gathering strength and focus from the drug. Thinking about that rich man's hunting lodge, the only place outsiders might be staying.

Her burning rage for her lost son. Her hatred of Bobby and Kinsey and everyone who was with them. It all came to them in a frenzied rush. But with the man's gun trained at them, all they could do was stand there.

Sherry glanced at her boyfriend. "I'll cover 'em, Luther. You take care of her." She trained her rifle sights in the direction of the SUV. Luther lowered his slightly and walked toward Kinsey. When he got close, he grabbed one of her arms. She struggled but he easily got her other arm and forced her on her stomach on the ground. He pulled a rope off his belt and bound her hands behind her back. Another piece of rope tied her feet together. Then he hauled her up to her knees.

Kinsey appeared to be in shock; her eyes were dull and glassy. That is, until Luther kicked her in the ribs. She made a wheezing sound and her eyes cleared; she looked around with panic as if just realizing where she was and what was happening.

"What'd you do to Jimmy, bitch?" the man said. "What'd you do to her son?"

"Nothing!" Kinsey said. "It's not our fault!" She continued urgently, words tumbling over one another. "Listen, we're, like, victims too. It's the government—they gave us this thing and it's killing all of us. We're all going to die in a few days anyway—just let us go so we can spend our last bit of life in peace."

Sherry had been listening in horror. "No!" she screeched. "Don't you say that! My son is not going to die. You tell us what you did and how we can fix it!"

The trio trapped by the car noticed her gun had lost its fixed aim in their direction. "We could get to the house!" Marla thought frantically. "There are guns inside!"

"She'll shoot us!" Diane's terrified mind responded.

"They're going to kill us anyway—we're witnesses," Lars pointed out. "We've got to try. It's our only chance—and Kinsey's."

They heard Kinsey's thoughts, overcome by the throbbing pain in her chest but willing them to go.

"Okay," Marla thought. "Ready? Go!" She darted toward the house, pulling Diane by one hand. Lars sprinted after them.

They heard a click of a rifle being cocked, and Diane shrieked a little, breathlessly, but they pounded up the steps of the lodge. Marla grappled desperately with the door, got it open, and pulled Diane inside, with Lars on their heels, just as a gunshot rang out.

CHAPTER FOURTEEN

"Got you, you little bastard," Luther said. For a panic-stricken moment, the trio thought one of them had been shot, but then the killer's thoughts reached them. They realized Bobby had started to crawl toward them and Luther had shot him again.

Kinsey screamed, a mournful sound that pierced the trio's hearts. "Come on," Marla thought, slamming the deadbolt shut. She pounded back to the rear part of the first floor, where the gun cabinet was.

Thankfully it wasn't locked. They got it open and pulled down rifles. "How do we load these?" Diane thought.

"Not sure, but make sure you don't point them at anyone while we're trying to figure it out," thought Lars.

"Fuck it, I'm going to bluff," Marla thought, hoisting hers awkwardly onto her shoulder. She went back to the front of the cabin. Using the butt of the rifle, she pounded against the glass of one of the front windows until it cracked and then shattered. She poked the muzzle through the jagged hole.

"Hey!" she shouted. "Motherfuckers! You let her go now, or I start shooting!"

The man and woman looked up, then moved quickly to the SUV. They opened the passenger side door and crouched behind it.

From there, they started firing at her. She spun away from the window and pressed against the wall. "Be careful guys!" she shouted silently.

"Got it!" Lars said aloud. "Diane, get down—I don't want you to get hit." Diane obeyed unhesitatingly, dropping her still-empty rifle.

Lars raced toward the front window. A bullet smashed another hole in the window and narrowly missed him. He dropped to an awkward crawl, holding the heavy rifle in one hand. It dragged and bumped along the floor and he offered a silent desperate request to the universe that it not discharge accidentally.

He reached Marla and knelt up to peer out the window. She too moved so she could see what was going on outside. He cocked his rifle, squinting, and fired one shot toward the SUV. It hit the car door with a dull thudding sound, but the sound of the gun discharging in the lodge was deafening. Lars shook his head ineffectually to try to clear the ringing in his ears.

There was no answering shot immediately. Lars hesitated, his gun still trained on the door of the car.

Just then, Kinsey managed to get to her feet. Her ankles still bound, arms tied behind her back, she started to hop awkwardly toward the lodge.

"Stay where you are, you little bitch!" Sherry's voice shrilled from her hiding place. Kinsey kept going, her brow furrowed in concentration, her body threatening to lose its balance with every clumsy landing.

Luther stepped from behind the SUV door, aimed quickly and expertly, and fired.

Kinsey stopped, floundered for a moment, her expression bewildered, then fell face down onto the gravel. They could hear her moaning faintly.

"Oh my god!" Marla said in a quavering voice. But Lars had kept his eyes fixated on the SUV. He squeezed the trigger.

The man bellowed. Lars fired again and he fell to the ground. Sherry screamed and flung herself on top of him. "Baby!" she cried. She looked toward the lodge and the thoughts they could sense in her mind were terrible. She stood up with her gun and started walking forward, cocking and firing. Shots whistled and thudded wildly into the wall and door of the house. Lars aimed and fired but his shot went wild.

The woman reached Kinsey's writhing body. She paused. Her eyes were wide, the look on her face savage. She pointed her gun down and stuck it against the back of Kinsey's head. Marla whimpered helplessly as she watched.

Sherry's shot and Lars's rang out nearly simultaneously. Kinsey spasmed just as Sherry fell down next to her. Lars fired again and the woman stopped moving.

There was sudden silence. Lars watched for a few more moments to see if he could detect any movement from either the man or woman. There was nothing.

Diane's mind was a confusion of horror. Marla put her gun down and helped her up, her arm around the girl's shaking shoulders.

Lars finally put his rifle down, carefully. They felt a chasm of guilt in his mind at having killed two people, and at not being able to save Kinsey. The girls ran to him and flung their arms around him and the three of them held one another for a long time. When they finally let go, Lars looked out the window again. No one had moved. He could see pools of blood seeping from under Kinsey and Sherry. Bobby and Luther's bodies hadn't moved. Lars's shoulders slumped.

* * *

The adrenaline drained from the trio's bodies. With silent agreement, they headed to the girls' bedroom and got into bed fully clothed. Lars said aloud, "Even if we survive this, I'll always have to live with killing two human beings." He shook his head. "I'm a fucking vegetarian. I've never even thrown a punch."

The girls pressed against him, and he kissed one, then the other, fiercely. Like the first time they'd kissed, all their cheeks were wet with tears, their throats achy. He buried his head in Diane's neck and sobbed. They pressed as close together as possible.

They slipped back into speaking with their minds. It was actually easier than trying to talk through the lumps in their throats.

"Nobody is going to believe we didn't cause all of this," Marla thought.

"We have to find somewhere to hide," Diane said. But none of them could think of where to go or even how to get away.

Even with the sun streaming through the window, the trio drifted off to sleep, a restless slumber punctuated by increasingly disturbing dreams. About an hour later, Lars's nightmare spread to all of their minds. They sat up, sweaty and disoriented. They exchanged kisses, but they were all thinking with cold dread of the three bodies in the shed and four more in front of the lodge.

The house was large and quiet with just the three of them in it. Downstairs, Diane brewed a pot of coffee while they communed silently.

"The car is still our best hope," Lars thought. Images flashed through his—and therefore the girls'—mind of the bullet holes in the body and windshield. "If it still runs, we can use it to get to a bus station."

"A big city, where we can disappear," Marla thought. "New York?"

Diane made a noise between a laugh and a sob. "I was going to go to college near there in the fall," she thought.

Marla stroked her hand. "We might be able to get back to our normal lives at some point," she said aloud, though they knew she didn't believe it.

"New York it is," Lars thought, changing their line of thinking. "We aren't going to get that thing started without keys though. And we need money."

Marla began another search for the keys, more methodically this time. Diane hunted for money and anything of value. Lars gathered quilts and comforters and went outside. Diane sensed what he wanted to do and went with him. "I'll look in everybody's pockets," she thought, feeling a fresh wave of horror but also determined to pull her weight today.

They went to the closest bodies, Kinsey's and Sherry's. Diane held her breath and lightly touched the woman's pockets one by one. She found nothing except a set of keys. She pulled them out with a flare of hope, then a quick letdown. There was no car in sight and they didn't remember hearing one; they hadn't heard any cars except their own while at the lodge since they'd gotten there. Lester and Sherry could have parked anywhere within a mile, in any direction. She pocketed the keys, though, just in case they came across it by chance.

Kinsey was in sweats and had nothing on her. Lars covered each body with a blanket. They moved on to the man's body by the car. Diane crouched and gingerly reached into a bulging hip pocket of jeans that smelled as if they hadn't been washed in a month. She pulled out a wallet and found a few wrinkled twenties, which she plucked out, and then moved to his front pockets. She produced a glass pipe and a small baggie of crystals. She held them up to Lars questioningly. "Ice," he thought.

After a moment of hesitation, she pocketed the baggie. "Guess it might be worth something," she thought.

They covered the man and moved to Bobby. His body was frozen in a grisly midcrawl position with one arm stretched out in front of him and one bent close to his body. Diane shivered as she knelt beside him.

She found his wallet in the hip pocket of his jeans. Her eyes widened as she pulled out a sheaf of hundreds as well as some smaller bills. He also had several credit cards, but she left them—probably linked to his parents, and also traceable by the government, she thought.

She rooted through his other pants pockets and found a lighter that looked expensive, so she took it. Then she dug through his jacket pockets. Her mouth dropped open. Completely forgetting for a moment that she'd just pulled it from the pocket of a corpse, she cried out and brandished the car key in the air.

CHAPTER FIFTEEN

Marla had caught Diane's triumphant thoughts from inside the lodge. She ran out to Diane and Lars, and the three of them hugged tightly.

Lars covered Bobby up, quickly growing somber again though still awash with relief, and looked over the SUV. Aside from a bullet hole in the passenger side door and some cracks in the windshield, it was in good condition.

They searched the car and found an envelope with more money in it in the glove compartment. All told, they had about a thousand dollars.

They went back inside to pack, and Marla showed them what else she'd unearthed in Bobby's room—an ounce or so of pot, a small baggie with a tiny amount of coke, and another with fifteen small white pills. Lars scraped one lightly and touched his fingernail to his tongue. He made a face. "I think it's molly," he said.

They stashed the drugs in various parts of their suitcases, along with their clothes and other belongings. After much consideration, they decided to leave all phones and tablets behind, afraid they could be tracked. Then they made a final pass through the rooms, picking up toiletries, the last of the food, and other incidentals.

Diane cried out in surprise from the kitchen, her thoughts too confused and scattered to read, and the other two hurried from the rooms they were in.

She pointed a shaking finger at her mug on the counter. A puddle of coffee surrounded it.

"What's wrong?" Marla asked aloud, anxiously.

Diane looked at her with eyes wide. "I started thinking I wanted a cup of coffee. All of a sudden, it felt as if my mind and the pot were connected, like I was pulling it toward me. I turned around and the coffee pot was floating in the air toward my cup. It was like—I don't know—like I was rearranging the molecules around it." She laughed, sounding incredulous at her own words. "The pot tipped over like it was trying to pour coffee into my mug. It went everywhere, but it was amazing. Then I put it back—" She pointed over to the coffeemaker, where the carafe was sitting in its place. She looked up at them again. "I don't know what happened, but I did it somehow!"

There was nothing in Diane's head to indicate she was joking. Marla and Lars shared the terrible thought that she was heading into a delusional state already.

"No, it's real, I swear!" Diane said. That made them relax somewhat; Rose and Bobby had lost their psychic powers when the other symptoms set in.

"Look, let me try to move something else." She looked around, smiled, and closed her eyes in concentration. The buttons of Marla's shirt stirred one by one, then slipped out of the buttonholes. Marla looked down, stunned. Lars laughed disbelievingly. Diane opened her eyes and grinned at them. Marla's shirt went limp and she rebuttoned it absentmindedly.

"That's . . . amazing," Lars managed at last. His curiosity bloomed. He focused on Diane's cup. Slowly it wobbled off the counter and toward him. He reached out and grabbed it, sloshing a bit more coffee.

"Holy shit!" Marla said. She glanced around. A magazine lying on a side table in the living room lifted itself into the air. Slowly, haltingly, it opened and the pages started turning, one by one.

For the next hour or so, they practiced their newfound powers. They opened the front door and took their belongings to the car using only their minds. Diane pushed the button on the key while it was still in her pocket to unlock the car, then opened the doors and trunk and loaded their luggage and supplies into the car. They soon figured out how to triangulate their minds on a single task; they had more control and power together, which helped with heavier items or more intricate tasks. Lars tested his range by focusing on a tree and plucking pinecones that were barely visible from where they stood. He brought the cones through the air and dropped them gently on the ground in front of him.

Despite the circumstances, it was thrilling. They'd gone from having no hope and no idea how to leave to having a working vehicle, money, and powers they could barely believe were real. As they marveled silently at the turn of fortune, Lars picked up Diane and swung her around, then planted a kiss on Marla's lips. "And I guess I suddenly have two amazing girlfriends," he said, sounding bashful. Diane and Marla both melted at the word. He didn't have to say what he was thinking; they went back into the house holding hands.

In the living room he stopped. "I guess we're alone here now," he said. A shadow crossed his face, but his thoughts quickly shifted as the girls started kissing him. "This is still unbelievable," he breathed, fumbling to undress them. "If we couldn't read each other, I'd wonder if you were playing some kind of joke on me." He pulled them onto the couch with him. "Knowing you both really do want this. . . ." He lost his train of thought and leaned his head against the back of the couch as Marla unbuttoned his shirt and started kissing his chest and belly. His hand stroked her back; his other hand laced its fingers through Diane's curls.

Diane broke off what she was doing and looked up at them, her eyes wide and questioning. "What was that?" she thought.

The fog of pleasure cleared. They dressed quickly while turning their minds, like positioning a satellite or antenna, to the other presences they suddenly sensed.

Imagery flashed into their minds first; it was as if they were inside other people, looking out through their eyes. Crawling through grass, climbing down hillsides, checking firearms, peering through binoculars. Studying controls on what appeared to be a plane—no, a helicopter, they all agreed as they felt its peculiar movement. Looking at the lodge from different vantage points.

Then they could sense what was being said. "The building is in sight. No sign of the subjects." "Are those bodies? Looks like four bodies in front of the place." "No living subjects spotted yet."

The three exchanged thoughts quickly, sometimes simultaneously, so it was impossible to pinpoint where ideas originated as they pieced together what was happening. They realized that the people surrounding them didn't know two of the bodies weren't from their group and thought there was only one person left alive. But they weren't sure how it could help them.

By then, they were dressed. The fleeting feeling of freedom they'd had a moment earlier had vanished.

They came together in a kind of three-sided hug, pressing together, wondering if it was all over. Diane whimpered in abject fear, Marla's mind was starting to withdraw into a resigned stillness, and Lars was tormented at the thought of having his chance at love snatched away so soon after finding it.

"It's not fair, it's not fair." Their minds echoed with his thought, over and over. Lars opened his eyes and his gaze fixed at random on the coffee pot. He felt his mind closing around it. He clenched with anger. The pot shattered into hundreds of pieces, coffee flying everywhere, dripping down the counter and onto the floor.

The girls jerked around, surprised by the sudden crashing sound. They looked at the coffee dripping down as if hypnotized. Then at each other.

CHAPTER SIXTEEN

First, they practiced. There was a ceiling fan overhead. They turned it on with their minds. Focusing together on the blades, they managed to slow them down and eventually bring them to a standstill.

Diane worried that it would be harder with a more distant object they couldn't see. Marla thought, "But we can see them. We can see through their eyes."

So they focused. Together they focused on one sniper at a time, on his gun. They searched through it for delicate mechanisms, parts none of them knew the terms for or even their exact function, and bent them, separated them, snapped them in two. They worked on minute pieces. The snipers holding the guns noticed nothing.

One after another, they worked on the weapons together. They lost count of how many, close to twenty. The last one they turned to was the sniper in the helicopter.

They searched for more, but they seemed to have gotten to them all. They doubted whether they'd really managed to disable the guns and keep them from firing. But they also realized that the agents were creeping ever closer. Soon someone would attempt to check the truck, enter the building, and it would be more than a case of overcoming weaponry. They might have to try to fight physically. All three were horrified at the idea of trying to use their powers on people's bodies.

They glanced around the main living area one last time for anything obvious they needed to take with them. They saw nothing. "Ready?" Marla thought. They stood by the door and took deep breaths, tensing their bodies.

Their minds flung the door open and they ran the short distance to the Suburban.

They piled in, Lars at the wheel with Marla in the passenger side and Diane in the back seat. They felt the ripple of alarm as the agents tried and failed to fire warning shots. The spreading confusion as they radioed one another and discovered they were all having the same issue with their weapons.

They could hear the helicopter clearly now that they were outside. As Lars fumbled to start the SUV, it dropped even lower, hovering over the tops of the tall pine trees. The pilot was assessing the best place to land.

Lars got the vehicle started and jammed it into reverse. He screeched backward in a semicircle until he was facing the narrow, rocky path up the hill and out of the hollow.

The helicopter buzzed closer to them. "We have to stop them from landing!" Marla thought. Diane remembered the practice run on the ceiling fan. The two girls focused on the much larger blades of the helicopter. They pressed against them. They could hear the blades scream in resistance. The helicopter swerved and tilted wildly. Then, as if just realizing how improbable it was that such a heavy, ungainly piece of machinery was flying at all, it lurched downward in free fall.

The blades hit first and churned the ground about twenty feet behind them, and they all felt the impact through the ground. Huge chunks of grass and soil thudded against the back of the SUV as it took off. The sounds of glass breaking and metal rending filled the air.

Lars drove as fast as he safely could up the steep rocky road. As they approached the first stand of trees the path wound through, an agent jumped out at them, grasping at and nearly clutching the driver's side mirror. Lars swerved away and the agent lost his balance, falling dangerously close to the wheels of the SUV.

They sensed more coming down the hill in a vehicle, in response to desperate radio calls. Diane and Marla focused on the brakes of the other truck, slowing it down. They disabled the passengers' guns and then the vehicle's engine.

They felt the passengers' confusion as the truck lost control.

They jolted up the hill and passed the vehicle they'd just tampered with, lying on its side not far from the road with smoke coming from under the hood. After that, they detected no other thoughts; they were free and clear, at least for the moment.

They continued driving, but by mutual agreement went in a different direction at the fork that would have taken them to the town they'd visited once with Derek. They drove for nearly an hour before coming across a town of sorts; just a gas station, a store, and a bar, with a scattering of homes that were slightly closer together than the ones they'd been passing sporadically.

The gas station had already closed, though it was barely five o'clock, but they saw a rusty phone booth outside by a soft drink vending machine. They pulled over and Marla got out; on a metal shelf under the phone itself was a slim phone book. It covered several ZIP codes and had an even smaller yellow pages section.

Marla flipped through it until she found a listing for a Greyhound bus station. There was one about fifty miles away, according to a map they'd found in the glove compartment of the Suburban. They got back on the road and used the map to get to it without too many wrong turns.

While the other two waited outside in the car, Diane went in to see about fares. They followed her thoughts in there and so knew how it had gone before she returned, close to tears. Three tickets to New York City would run them close to three hundred dollars, and the next bus didn't leave until the next morning.

"Well, that's out," Lars thought glumly. "It'd chew up a third of our money, and we'd have to hang out here overnight. They'll be looking for us in every nearby town."

"I guess we just drive this thing as far as we can and hope no one spots us," Marla thought grimly.

Diane had grabbed a timetable from the station, and by studying travel times they decided to set their sights on Pittsburgh instead of New York. After they passed through another small town, they came across an old truck for sale by owner. It sat at the end of a long driveway and they saw no one in the yard or windows of the house. They pulled over and Lars swapped license plates with it, using a screwdriver found in a toolbox in the back section of the Suburban.

An hour or so later they crossed the state border into Pennsylvania. It was a meaningless milestone, but they all felt a bit freer nonetheless.

At a truck stop about twenty miles away from Pittsburgh, they parked in a remote corner. Lars went to get them food in the service center, his ball cap pulled low over his forehead to shield his face as well as he could from security cameras. They ate hurriedly in the car. Their surroundings seemed surreal after having spent so many nights at the lodge.

Soon Pittsburgh was in sight. In their shell-shocked state, they hadn't talked or thought in any organized fashion that morning, but as they neared their hastily chosen destination, they started to communicate more. Their first thought was to find somewhere to stay.

"I've got my fake ID," Lars said. "I can probably just reserve a hotel room with that, pay with cash, if it's a smaller place."

They drove over a bridge and toward the skyline, dramatic and refreshing after days and days of seeing nothing but trees, hills, and farmhouses. Lars drove aimlessly, keeping an eye out for a cheap hotel. They found one in a neighborhood with signs of neglect: more litter strewn on the streets, graffiti on rusty metal doors. The hotel had a neon sign and cracked steps leading up to it. They parked in a small lot next to it.

Inside, a bored, heavyset man with a stubbly face checked them in. "Sixty a night, pay in advance every night, or three-fifty for a week," he said.

"Just one night," Diane thought, shivering at the forlorn interior of the lobby.

The room was dingy, with dirty windows, a stained comforter on the double bed, and threadbare carpeting. The bathroom was grim too, with a rusty residue around each of the drains and dirt along the corners of the sink and tub. The trio sat down on the bed together, skin crawling too much to lie down, and cuddled while they thought together.

"We can't stay here for long," Diane thought with a shudder.

"If we went somewhere better, we'd use up our money faster," Marla countered.

"If we stay here, we'll probably get robbed anyway, and maybe killed in the process."

Lars thought, "Don't forget we can defend ourselves."

"But we've never used it on people. We don't know what would happen," Diane said aloud.

"We might have to try someday," Marla said.

"At least we'll be able to tell who's a threat before anything happens," Diane conceded.

The three ventured out onto the street to raise money, walking in a tight-knit cluster. They got some looks but everyone they passed seemed to have their minds on something other than robbing or hurting them.

They walked through dark alleys between buildings and stood on street corners, and read the thoughts of everyone they passed. Eventually they started finding people who had money and a desire to buy drugs. They sold the molly for twenty dollars a pill, the meth for forty and the minute baggie of coke for thirty.

They passed a pawn shop and stopped in to sell Bobby's lighter; the owner offered twenty-five and they could tell from his thoughts that he wouldn't go any higher, so they settled for that.

They headed back out with only the baggie of weed left, searching minds, until they came across a prospective customer. The man was white but wore his graying hair in long, messy dreadlocks. They approached him.

"Looking to buy something?" Lars asked.

The man looked at him, and they could hear him sizing up the situation and the three kids. He sensed no threat and nodded, smiling cautiously.

"Let's go over there," Lars said, craning his neck to a small dark space between two buildings. The man hesitated but complied.

Diane produced the baggie. "Two hundred?" she said. The man touched it, assessed the amount, and agreed.

As he was counting out his money, he asked, "What are you kids doing out here anyway?"

They hesitated and conferred silently. "Just hit a rough patch," Lars said. "Trying to survive, basically."

The man's thoughts were sympathetic. The drugs and money exchanged hands. "Ran away?" They all nodded hesitantly. "All together?" he asked. Again, they nodded.

"I've had some rough times too," he said. "Until I learned how to just drop out of it altogether. The whole rat race."

"Wish we knew how to do that," Diane said.

The man smiled again. "Hey, do you want to come hang out with me for a few days?" he asked. "It's not much, but I've got some blankets and an old mattress you could use." The trio paused cautiously. They searched his mind and found only kindness.

"That would be great," Marla said. "Only—do you live with a bunch of other people? We kind of need to keep a low profile."

"Nope, just me," he said. "My lady friend's taking a break from me right now. I wouldn't mind the company."

They walked back to the hotel together. The trio gathered their things from their room and checked out. The clerk was utterly uninterested beyond reminding them that there were no refunds.

They walked out. Lars pointed to the car and said, "That's ours, so we could drive to where you are."

"Great!" the man said, pleased and surprised. "It's only a couple miles away, but takes about half an hour on the bus—when it comes."

They got in. Lars conferred with the girls and said, "We should probably park it a ways away though. It's—we borrowed it from—my dad, so just in case he's looking for us. . ."

"Understood," the man said. "I'll show you a pretty safe place to park that's a few blocks from where I stay."

They parked the car, grabbed their things, and followed the man down the street. He introduced himself as Markie and they gave hastily altered names. He gestured to a café that they were passing. "This is where I get breakfast almost every day," he said. "Tastiest trash in the city." He laughed.

They could read the explanation in his mind before he finished saying it. "I'm a freegan," he said. "I mostly dumpster-dive my meals. I only buy food if I absolutely need to, and most of the time I don't.

"Believe me, it's not gross," the man added, not needing to read their minds to figure out what they were thinking. "A lot of stuff gets tossed still in containers. And veggies can all be washed and cooked, so they're fine."

"Well," said Lars, "Is it okay for you to eat food that's bought, if someone else buys it?"

The man laughed. "Sure; I never turn down hospitality. I give freely of what I have, and if others want to do that as well, I accept it."

"Well, we'll be happy to treat you to dinner at that place tonight," Lars said. "We'll be saving so much money not being in the hotel."

"If I go with you, you have to promise to let me cook for you tomorrow," the man said. "C'mon, you have to at least try it."

The trio glanced at each other reluctantly. But they couldn't resist the abundant kindness of the man's thoughts. "Okay," Diane said.

He laughed again and clapped her on the back. "It's a deal," he said.

CHAPTER SEVENTEEN

They stopped in front of a two-story building with peeling paint and boarded windows. If they hadn't been able to read minds so clearly, they never would have set foot in such a building, especially not after dark and with a complete stranger.

The man led them around back, where three concrete stairs led up to a door with a board across it. He tugged at the board until two nails came out of well-worn holes in the end closest to the doorknob, and rotated the board down, still attached with one nail on the other end. He yanked on the door and it came open without having to turn the knob; they saw there was no latch or else it had been permanently stuck inside the door.

Markie swung it open and they stepped into darkness. Markie groped for a candle and lit it. In the dim light they could see they were in a dingy stairwell with stairs leading both up and down. He took them upstairs and through another ruined door.

He lit more candles. The room they stepped into, a kitchen, was worn but clean.

"No running water," he said. "I fill up bottles whenever I'm somewhere with a sink, so I've got some, but use it sparingly." He gestured proudly to a metal contraption sitting on top of the electric stove. "No electricity either. That's my propane burner. Always open the window if you're gonna use it. Actually, ask me if you want to use it first so I can show you all the tricks. You'll be amazed what I can make with that!"

Markie led them into the next room, which was nearly empty except for a few boxes, a broken bike with tools lying around it, and a small table with a couple of mismatched chairs. "Dining room, kind of," he said with a smile.

The room after that was the living area, surprising cozy given how the exterior of the building looked. A saggy sofa and an armchair, both covered with faded quilts, surrounded a scratched coffee table. Along the wall, several milk crates stacked on top each other held a motley assortment of well-used books.

There were no lamps or any other electrical devices, but there were candles on every surface, in mason jars and on foil pie plates, molded to the windowsill with motionless rivers of congealed wax.

"Your room is back this way—you mind all sleeping in the same room?" he interrupted himself to ask.

Diane went scarlet and the other two grinned sheepishly. "No, we don't mind," Marla said.

The man nodded knowingly and led them to a door that more or less closed. He opened it to reveal a mattress with a hole-riddled sheet and a threadbare comforter folded at the foot of it. A slightly crooked footstool with a couple more candles melted onto it sat by the side. Like the other rooms it looked shabby but clean.

"This is the guest room," Markie said with self-deprecating fake grandeur. "It's just a double bed but you should be able to squeeze into it, I think."

"Thank you so much," Diane said with genuine gratitude.

"God yes," Marla said. "This is so much better than that hotel room we wasted our money on."

The man grinned shyly. He led them back out and showed them the bathroom. "You can pee in the toilet, but if you can wait when you need to take a shit, there's a few places with public bathrooms nearby. If you absolutely can't, don't worry; I know a nice guy that'll lend me a bucket of water from time to time." Markie smiled. "I do mending for him sometimes so it works out."

The trio smiled back at him, strangely charmed. "Put your toilet paper in this bag" —

he indicated a loosely tied plastic shopping bag lying by the toilet. "I take care of it every few days. The sink doesn't work but my lady bought this hand sanitizer, so you can use that." He pointed to a clear plastic bottle with a push dispenser. "We can use the bathtub if we cart water in from my neighbor. Luckily he's in construction and works on cars; he always needs mending done," he said with a chuckle.

The only other room on the floor was his bedroom, which had a futon mattress, a beanbag chair, another crate of books, and more candles.

Markie made a flourish with his hands. "That's my home!" he said happily. "Until someone kicks me out. But I've been here for almost a year, and so far so good."

"It's amazing what you've done," Diane said. "And you got all this stuff for free?"

"Mostly, or traded it for something. Occasionally I do have to buy something. I do odd jobs once in a while, which is how I got the money for the weed." He snapped his fingers.

"That reminds me! Should we smoke up before we go out for dinner?"

"Yes please!" said Lars eagerly, then looked a bit guiltily at the girls. "Is that okay?" he thought at them. Marla shrugged and smiled.

They followed Markie back to the living room and the trio curled up on the couch while the man sat on the armchair. He leaned forward and took a box from the shelf under the coffee table, then began to roll a joint.

"So," Markie said as he worked, "you guys seem pretty close. Like you have a pretty deep connection." The trio looked at one another, stifling giggles. "Does that have anything to do with why you're running away?"

They sobered up quickly. Silently they conferred about whether to tell Markie their story, but they unanimously agreed they couldn't. "It has a little bit to do with it," Lars said. He fell silent.

"Hey, it's totally cool," Markie said. "I didn't mean to bring you down. People drop out for all kinds of reasons. You don't have to tell me anything you don't want to talk about."

"Thanks," Diane said, relieved. "It's hard."

"Well," the man said, "it may look like I go out of my way to do things the hard way, but actually I'm all about things being easier. So I want you three to take it easy while you're staying with me." He finished the joint, lit it, took a hit, and passed it around.

* * *

Marla and Diane had been apprehensive about letting their guard down, and about how the pot would affect them now with their newfound powers. Lars was much more experienced with the drug and not as worried, but even he wondered if anything would happen. But they all felt they needed to let everything go for a little while.

So they did. They walked the couple of blocks back to Markie's favorite diner pleasantly stoned. The staff knew him on sight and clearly didn't mind that he ate from their dumpster normally; they teased him and let the group buy beers without carding them. Markie and the trio had giant burritos and hearty hot sandwiches, with pie and coffee for dessert.

Recognizing that the three were still feeling guarded about their own pasts, Markie regaled them with stories of his own. They laughed harder than they had in weeks.

They stumbled back to the squat, feeling full, warm, and carefree. Markie, sensing they wanted to be alone, retired to his bedroom with a candle, saying he wanted to read.

Soon making out on the couch wasn't enough, and they blew out all the candles in the living room except one, which they took to find the way to their bedroom. Making love by candlelight seemed to intensify their feelings and physical sensations. For the first time they said aloud something that had stolen into their shared thoughts occasionally, but which they'd tried not to acknowledge reading in the others' minds. "I love you." Once they started saying it, they found it impossible to stop repeating it.

"Jackpot!" Markie's voice echoed inside the dumpster he was leaning into. His head appeared as he straightened up, both hands clutching full plastic containers of strawberries. He passed them down to Lars and Marla, who inspected them before placing them carefully into canvas bags already bulging with previous finds.

It was Marla's first time accompanying the men on a dumpster-diving expedition, and they'd had a good haul that day; day-old doughnuts, half a large takeout container of white rice, potatoes sprouting eyes all over, and some limp carrots and celery that Markie swore would perk right up if they submerged them in water.

As he jumped off the crate he'd been standing on to reach inside the garbage bin, Markie was already bragging about the amazing vegetable soup and strawberry doughnut dessert he was going to make for them that evening. He'd cooked nearly every meal for them the past couple weeks, with Diane increasingly helping out. They'd barely needed to touch their cash supply except to buy the occasional pack of toilet paper or jug of drinking water.

They'd quickly become accustomed to living with Markie. He was intuitive and could generally divine their moods. They had it much easier and could read exactly when he needed alone time or craved company.

His unspoken acceptance made the trio much less self-conscious about what was to them an unprecedented arrangement. They'd become reticent about public demonstrations of affection once they learned how much attention it attracted. But at Markie's squat, they were free to be open, and so the run-down house felt like a paradise.

By now they were masters at using their psychic powers unobtrusively. It was harder to flex the telekinesis in ways that wouldn't scare anyone. Occasionally, if they were alone, they'd practice, just to see if they could still do it. Though the siege at the lodge seemed at times like a distant dream, they never stopped wondering if they'd be found and need to fight their way free again. But as the days passed, they began to hope they'd gotten away for good.

Another fear had begun to ebb, as they outlived Rose and showed none of the symptoms she and Bobby had exhibited. They marveled about it sometimes, but they were also tormented by the thought that their other friends may have survived if they'd thought they had a chance. It still haunted them, wondering whether it would have given Monique the strength to keep from taking her own life, whether they could have helped

Sherry by telling her that her son might recover, and possibly saved her life as well as Bobby's, Kinsey's, and Lester's.

They tried not to dwell on what had happened, but they devoured headlines on newspapers as they passed corner dispensers, and stood riveted whenever they passed a television that had "breaking" running across the bottom of the screen. Nothing ever appeared about the mysterious outbreak at their school, or the massacre at the lodge.

* * *

That night, a shared dream pushed them toward consciousness. In it, they were reading Markie's panicked thoughts. He was frantically wishing he could shrink away from a knife held to his throat by a strange man, but he was being held in such a way that he couldn't move. His captor's mind was harder to read; they could detect his presence, but no clear thoughts came through to them.

It wasn't their first collective nightmare about being found, but it was different from the ones that had come before. Usually the recurring storyline was a recreation of the scene in West Virginia but in the streets of Pittsburgh. Bringing a helicopter down, watching its blades smash apartment windows and its body crush cars on impact. Trying to disable sniper rifles positioned on the rooftops around them as they ran down the street, dodging a gauntlet of gunshots. Sensing a seemingly endless army of faceless people with weapons all directed at the trio.

This time, they were in darkness, unable to see anything except what they could visualize through Markie's thoughts about what he was seeing. They sensed more minds than Markie's and the stranger's, but their thoughts were faint and hard to decipher, as if they were several blocks away.

Then they were awake, unmistakably out of the dream. And Markie's thoughts continued.

Their own minds were a tangle of confused questions and cold fear. They struggled to a sitting position on the mattress, the old quilt seeming to clutch at their sleep-weakened limbs, and then to standing.

In the gloom, Marla put her finger to her lips, though they could already tell from her thoughts that she wanted them to be quiet. She moved toward the door and leaned her head against it to listen. She could hear Markie's voice, strained and slightly shaky, talking in a low tone. She couldn't make it out but the trio knew what he was saying from his mind. Pleading with someone to let him go and talk to him. Underneath that was a rising tide of concern for them; he was keeping his voice quiet in hopes of defusing the situation without waking them and putting them in danger.

They stood frozen with indecision. If they tried to wrest the knife out of the assailant's hand with their minds, there was a strong possibility it would inflict damage to Markie as it moved. Their powers weren't precise enough to be sure they'd leave him unscathed.

Did the stranger know they were in the building too? His thoughts were inscrutable, like nothing they'd ever encountered before.

They couldn't glean anything about who he was or why he was doing this.

Then, as clear as if he were speaking aloud, his mind projected one unmistakable thought: Marla, Diane, Lars. Come out now.

Lars swore under his breath, incredulous. Diane covered her mouth with her hand, eyes wide.

It was Marla who pressed her lips tightly together, squared her shoulders, and opened the door.

Even by candlelight, the man's pressed khakis and white shirt looked impossibly crisp and clean against his run-down surroundings. Markie knelt on the floor in front of him, knife at his throat. It still felt like a dream had come to life somehow. His face was nearly expressionless, his eyes calm as their gazes met, although they could hear his frantic mind. "They don't need to be involved in whatever this is," he said in his uncharacteristically quiet, strained voice.

The man ignored his words. "Hello," he said. "I'm Hector White. I'm Derek's dad. Please, sit."

The three of them clutched hands. They could hear his thoughts mirroring the words he was speaking, like a slight echo, something they'd grown used to in the past few weeks. What was unusual was not getting any of the unspoken thoughts that must be running through his head.

Lars found his voice first. "I'm so sorry about Derek," he said. "We tried to stop Bobby but …"

"I don't blame you anymore for what happened to Derek," Hector said calmly, cutting him off. "I blame his generosity in wanting to help his friends." Something unspoken almost emerged from his mind. The trio chased it with theirs but it was gone before they could decipher it.

"I'm not here about my son. I've come to tell you you're the first subjects to survive our experiment for more than a couple of weeks. You're also the only ones who've developed the abilities you have. We're very interested to learn more about them."

Hector shifted and leaned forward slightly on the sagging cushion. Diane's eyes flicked from his face to the knife blade, willing it not to sink into Markie's skin, though she was afraid to try and actually move it. But maybe she was unwittingly applying some resistance that Hector could sense, because he looked directly at her. "I'm perfectly aware that you could get away right now. That you could probably figure out a way to get your friend out of this predicament too. So the only hope I have is convincing you to come with me."

"If you want to talk to us, you let him go first," Marla said. After a quiet, tense moment, Hector nodded and released Markie. He scrambled away and pressed against a wall, clutching his throat. They could hear his warring thoughts, veering between wanting to flee or stay and try to help them. The trio had similarly conflicting feelings—wanting his comforting presence yet afraid what Hector would do to him.

"You better go," Marla said to him. He looked about to protest so she said, "We'll be all right—we know him." She heard him wondering if he should get help and said, "No, we don't need you to do that." His eyes flared in shock. She nodded at him. Befuddled, he slowly backed toward the door.

"Bye Markie," Diane said over a lump in her throat. There was a note of finality, though none of them knew what was going to happen.

"I'll—uh—be back later?" he said uncertainly. They all nodded, and he slipped out the door. They heard his sandaled feet thudding on the stairs—not running, but faster than he usually went down them.

After his footsteps faded and they heard the downstairs door slam, Hector spoke again. "First, I want to make sure you know that this—condition has virtually no survival rate. You three are the first of hundreds, and we have no idea if you're anomalies. Every time you encounter another person in your age group, you're potentially starting a deadly epidemic.

"Second, life on the run is incredibly stressful. Even though you could probably get away whenever we found you, you'd never be able to fully relax. Because we would never stop trying. Besides, you'd have to hide your capabilities from those around you, as well as, I gather, your rather unusual relationship that's developed." The trio squirmed a bit but said nothing.

"And third, I want to assure you that we have no intention of harming you. If you agree to come with me and help us try to learn more about you, we'll keep you absolutely safe and comfortable."

Hector folded his hands calmly and looked at each of them in turn. "So," he said. "What do you think?"

Hector was still and neutral, his brain revealing nothing. All they could hear were their own beating hearts and hopeless, circular thoughts. Try as they might, Hector's logic seemed impenetrable. They spun through scenarios together that all seemed to lead to the same few grim conclusions.

Marla nodded. "All right," she said. "We're done."

Hector stood. He seemed neither surprised nor especially elated. "You've made the right choice," he said.

A matte black sedan was parked outside the building. He opened the back door on the driver's side and they crawled in together.

The door shut with a quiet click and a few seconds later Hector got into the driver's seat. He started the car, which smelled practically antiseptic compared with where they'd been, and pulled out.

The now-familiar buildings slipped by, and the three leaned against one another in a sort of trance. They left the recognizable streets of Pittsburgh and got onto the interstate heading south. Then they were on their way to—where? Virginia? DC? They realized they didn't know. They searched Hector's mind, but it was futile.

Although they were heading in the general direction of home, their former lives, their families, and their senior year of high school seemed like a distant memory, strangely foreign to the people they had become just in the past month. They listlessly watched lights slip by as they entered a new phase of their life, as strange and unknowable as the last several had been.

The girls each clasped one of Lars's hands. He kissed each one in turn and pressed it against his cheek, eyes closed. Even in this situation, he could appreciate how lucky they were in this one respect.

Diane suddenly remembered something she'd only half paid attention to back in the apartment. The strange whisper of a thought in Hector's mind that had almost revealed itself to them. Marla and Lars followed along, puzzled, as she searched to grasp its meaning. Then a possibility surfaced, took hold in her brain. The other two repeated it in their minds, stunned. *"Derek's alive?"*